Merlin's Destiny

D E D I C A T I O N

For Joey and Mike—

a pair of bandits who should be
outlawed from golf

Merlin's Destiny

SIGMUND BROUWER

A DIVISION OF SCRIPTURE PRESS PUBLICATIONS INC.
USA CANADA ENGLAND

THE WINDS OF LIGHT SERIES

Wings of an Angel
Barbarians from the Isle
Legend of Burning Water
The Forsaken Crusade
A City of Dreams
Merlin's Destiny
Jester's Quest

Cover design by Mardelle Ayres
Cover illustration by Jeff Haynie
Photo by Dwight Arthur

ISBN: 1-56476-049-9

3 4 5 6 7 8 9 10 Printing/Year 97 96 95 94

VICTOR BOOKS
A division of SP Publications, Inc.
Wheaton, Illinois 60187

AUTHOR'S NOTE

The "Winds of Light" series follows the adventures of the boy warrior, Thomas of Magnus, whose tale begins in England in the early 1300s.

Thomas' story spans six volumes, though each book tells a complete tale. *Wings of an Angel,* the first book in the series, describes how the orphan Thomas—then 14 and old enough to be considered a man—conquered the kingdom of Magnus and released its village from murderous oppression. He is aided by the mysterious young woman, Katherine, whose adventures also unfold throughout the series. We also meet Sir William, a wandering knight; Tiny John, a young pickpocket; self-serving Waleran; and Isabelle, a mute slave girl.

The second volume of the story of Magnus *(Barbarians from the Isle)* tells how Thomas battled the powerful northern Scots. He then faced a far greater trial, one imposed by Druid false sorcerers who demanded Thomas join their secret group or lose his lordship and his castle. We meet the powerful Earl of York and learn more of Katherine and her companion, an old man with special knowledge and power.

A victory against the Druids enabled Thomas to keep Magnus, but as the third volume *(Legend of Burning Water)* reveals, his victory was only temporary. Posing as false priests, the Druids regained Magnus. Thomas was forced to flee and take desperate action, guided by strangers he dared not trust, who knew the truth behind Magnus. Helping Thomas battle the Priests of the Holy Grail were Robert of Uleran, Thomas' faithful sheriff and Gervase, a priest who loves God.

In the fourth book, *The Forsaken Crusade,* Thomas held ransom what he believed was his single last chance to regain Magnus. Yet he failed, lost his hostage Isabelle, and escaped England across dangerous seas to the Holy Land, accompanied by a puppy who had saved his life. In the Holy Land he again encountered the mysterious Katherine, whose path had crossed his own so often.

A City of Dreams began in St. Jean d'Acre, where Thomas and Katherine were reunited with the wandering knight, Sir William. In that ancient city, Thomas gained surprising knowledge of his past and future destiny. Because of this knowledge, he started a quest failed by many others before.

As *Merlin's Destiny* begins, Thomas has finally learned most of the story behind his childhood in a monastery, and also in whom he can really trust. Yet the battle is far from over. He and those who fight with him must return to England—armed with the results of his Holy Land quest—to win the final battle against the Druids.

Though St. Jean d'Acre existed in fact, those interested in ancient times should know that Magnus itself cannot be found in any history book. Nor can Thomas be found, nor others of his friends and foes. Yet many of the famous people and events found in this story shaped the times of that medieval world, as historians may easily confirm.

1

THOMAS
The Cave of Letters

FALL A. D. 1313

It did not seem real, the stillness of the morning air and the pastel contrasts of crowded and ancient stone buildings against olive green and brown mountains, all framed by pale blue sky. It did not seem real, the background of the babble of the streets beneath the gentle warmth of the sun. And it did not seem real, to be walking—slowly and calmly—among the people on the streets while soldiers hunted this quarter of Jerusalem from house to house, soldiers determined to capture and crucify them.

Thomas of Magnus wondered briefly if the pounding of his heart might give him and the two others away.

Crucifixion.

Could any death be more horrible for them? A wooden pole would first be placed into the ground, and a crosspiece fixed near the top to form a cross. Then, if they were fortunate, their arms would be roped to the crosspiece, not nailed. Thomas knew—should the Mameluke soldiers in pursuit choose to be merciful—that he and the two others with him would then quickly die of suffocation, because the weight of their bodies would shut off their air passages. But should it be deemed that their agony be prolonged upon the crosses, the soldiers would nail their arms and feet into the wood, thus providing support for the body and making suffocation impossible. Death then, would occur much more slowly, from shock or dehydration or exhaustion.

Shouts of soldiers broke above the babble of the streets as they swept from house to house. *How far behind were the soldiers? And how far ahead the gates?*

Thomas dared not lift his head to glance at their progress. His gray-blue eyes and fair skin would be too obvious to any onlookers, for it had been over a hundred years since Crusader knights had held the Holy City. Now, the *infidels*—Muslim conquerors—ruled, and Thomas needed to keep his face hidden by the cloth which was draped over his head and neck as protection against the sun.

The other two, Katherine and Sir William, walked in wide separation and far in front. To remain in a group of three would instantly give their presence away to any sharp-eyed soldier.

More shouts, and angry arguments as new houses were searched.

For a moment, Thomas let his mind wander as he imagined what a rabbit might feel, crouched and barely hidden among the grass with a hawk, circling overhead. Any sudden movement would draw the hawk's attention, just as surely as anything, but a pretended calm now would draw soldiers. Yet Thomas could understand why a rabbit might bolt under the strain of waiting beneath a hawk, even knowing that to bolt meant certain death. It took great effort to force himself to walk slowly when every nerve shrieked at him to run.

The stakes were enormous.

A terrible death through crucifixion mattered little in comparison to the scrolled map Katherine held in her travel pouch. He and the knight, Sir William, planned to fight to the death should they be discovered. And she was to escape while they fought. For without the scroll, a much greater battle—thousands of miles away—would be lost with cold certainty.

So much depended on escape from this city....

Thomas bit his tongue to keep those thoughts away. For he could not let fear paralyze him.

Instead, he directed his mind to the events which had led to this day, any thoughts at all except those of the soldiers in pursuit.

How long since he had been exiled from England? Already half a year. The great sweeping valleys of Magnus—lush green with the scattered purple patches of heather, and shrouded with mist in the winter—were an aching memory.

He had survived a cutthroat ship's crew, and a bandit-infested trek through the Holy Land. He had survived betrayals and lies, and now finally, just as he had established that he could trust the two with him, the soldiers were in pursuit....

Thomas shook his head. *Walk slowly and think not of the soldiers,* he told himself.

So he thought of Katherine, and the moment she had first lifted her face to his in silvery moonlight. He remembered how his heart had caught as if they had been long pledged for the moment, and how later, in the Holy Land, the mystery of that yearning had been explained. He thought of their first fleeting kiss, one of anger and frustration at desires neither could understand or trust. He thought of how candlelight bounced off her blonde hair, the curves of her face in the shadows of that candlelight, and her half-hinted smile of inner joy. He thought of the beauty of depth of character, the slow, measured way she would stare deeply into his eyes. If he were to lose her now, after all they had been through. . . .

Walk slowly and think not of the soldiers.

There was the knight, Sir William. Thomas need only close his eyes to see the knight as he remembered him from their first meeting at a gallows, long ago and far away. The rugged and handsome face of a man who had been a trained fighter his entire adult life. Darkly tanned, with hair—showing a trace of gray at the edges—cropped short. Blue eyes as deep as they were careful to hide thoughts. And a ragged scar down his right cheek. The knight had helped him win Magnus and much later, greeted him in the Holy Land. With his help again, they had this quest to fulfill. *Yet could Sir William's fighting skill and intelligence prove victorious against the Mameluke soldiers, a breed of fighters who had once defeated the Great Genghis Khan and his horde of Mongols?*

Again, those dreaded shouts. Nearer now.

Walk slowly and think not of the soldiers.

Activity on the narrow twisting streets still seemed normal, a small piece of good fortune for Thomas. Obviously the people of Jerusalem were accustomed to the sight of running soldiers, for despite the shouts that carried from street to street, the bartering and selling at market booths continued.

Thomas felt a tug on the edge of his cape.

"Alms for the poor?"

He looked down into raisin black eyes. A boy. Maybe six years old.

The boy's eyes widened as he noticed Thomas' European features. His mouth opened as he drew breath to speak his surprise.

"Alms you will have, my friend," Thomas said quickly to

forestall any exclamation. "But you must grasp my hand!"

The command intrigued the boy enough that he did so and remained silent.

"Your name?" Thomas asked, his head still low as he looked at the beggar.

"Addon. I am seven."

Another memory stabbed at Thomas. That of someone barely older than this boy. Tiny John, a pickpocket rascal as mischievous and cheerful as a sparrow, who might have already perished in England.

Thomas blocked the memory, and concentrated on walking slowly, holding the boy's hand as naturally as if they were brothers. For if the boy bolted now and spread the word of a pale-skinned stranger. . . .

"Addon, as you observed, I am a traveler, now confused and lost in this great city of yours. It will be worth a piece of gold if you guide me to the nearest city gate."

The boy grinned. "Essenes Gate! For a piece of gold."

Essenes Gate. As Thomas well knew, it was guarded by only one tower. Less than five mintues away, and well-marked in the mind of the knight in front of him. However, if a piece of gold and a feeling of self-importance kept this child silent until they had left the city walls. . . .

"After the gates, where shall I take you next?" the boy was asking.

"That shall suffice." Thomas smiled. This young guide wished to earn even more. "For then I depart."

Addon frowned. "Did you not know that is impossible?"

"Impossible?"

A quick nod from the young beggar. "The Mameluke soldiers have shut all the city gates. They guard them now."

2

"Addon, this is indeed your blessed day," Thomas said as slowly and calmly as possible. He could not afford to alarm the boy or raise his suspicions. "For you shall earn enough gold to feed you for a month."

Addon grinned happiness, his teeth a crescent of white against dark skin.

"There is a man ahead of me," Thomas continued in low tones. "See him yonder?"

Thomas pointed at Sir William until Addon nodded.

"Approach him, and tell him the same news you gave me. Tell him I shall wait here for his return."

Addon scampered ahead.

Thomas waited in the shadow of a doorway and watched Sir William's head bend as he listened to Addon, then watched with relief as the knight turned back. To any other but Thomas, it would have been impossible to notice that the knight spoke to a veiled woman as he passed her upon his return, for he did not pause and his lips barely moved. Yet, moments after the knight passed her, Katherine stopped where she was, then began to shuffle, to wait near a stand where a vendor shouted the sale of melons.

"Thomas," the knight said softly when he reached the doorway, "news of the gates does not bode well for us."

Thomas drew deeper in the shadows. "The Mamelukes must know not only of our presence, but of the scroll and the Cave of Letters. Why else go to such measures to find us?"

Sir William's lips tightened in anger. "A sword across the throat of the man who betrayed us—"

"Think of our throats," Thomas interrupted. "The city is sealed. Yet we cannot keep our faces hidden forever. It will be too difficult to remain unnoticed inside."

Sir William closed his eyes in thought. Moments later, he smiled. "Have you a thirst for spring water?"

"Water? We fight for our lives and—"

"Thomas, tell me of Jerusalem's history."

"There are soldiers all around! This is no place for—"

"Come, come," Sir William chided with a grin. "Surely as a Merlin you would have a glimmer of this knowledge."

Thomas snorted. "The city is as ancient as man. Its history would take hours to recite."

"Tell me then," the knight grinned, "of King David."

Despite the danger he felt pressing upon them, Thomas grinned in return. How many peaceful hours of his childhood had been spent in the same tests and discussions?

"King David?" Thomas squinted his eyes shut in thought. "King David. He chose this as his capital because it sat squarely between Israel in the north and Judah in the south. Yet until him, the city had never been conquered, for it held a spring and no siege could bring it down."

"Yes," Sir William said. "The spring. Gihon Spring."

Gihon Spring. Then Thomas knew. He grinned. "We shall

leave Jerusalem the same way it was conquered."

Thomas turned to Addon and spoke. "You must guide us to the inner city."

He did not finish his thoughts. *The inner city—close to the palace and soldiers quarters.*

The imposing structure of the palace lay in the background, and directly ahead, the circular area where three main streets joined. At the center of that large circle stood the well. Thomas surveyed the bulwark of bricked stones that surrounded the well and groaned. He could not share his dismay with anyone, because the knight and Katherine had—by necessity—traveled separately the entire journey back into the center of Jerusalem.

"You wish a different well?" Addon asked in response to the low groan. "Yet there is none more ancient—"

"No," Thomas said, "a better guide we could not have found."

That was truth. For Addon had led them through a maze of narrow and obscure alleyways which made detection by searching soldiers almost impossible. Ironic then, that the first soldiers they had seen would now surround the well.

Thomas bit back another groan.

A dozen solders were all within a stone's throw. More ironically, none were there as guards. Instead, they stood or sat in relaxed enjoyment of the sun and gossip. Around the well too were the reasons for the soldiers' presence—the women gathered to draw water from the well.

Their idle conversation reached Thomas clearly. He gnawed his inner lip as he lost himself in thought.

Gihon Spring. Once, long ago, the shepherd boy named

David who earned a reputation as a military genius and united all of Israel, had sent his soldiers up this well shaft to invade and conquer Jerusalem. *Was the shaft still clear after these hundreds of years?*

There was only one means of discovering the answer. They must descend.

But the soldiers stood between them and a desperate attempt at escape. Only a distraction could—

Shouts and the braying of donkeys interrupted his thoughts.

Thomas looked to his right in disbelief. Two donkeys plunged in frantic paths through the small market on a nearby sidestreet. The donkeys careened through stands of fruits and beneath the awnings which provided shade. One donkey plunged back out again, draped in the blankets from a shop.

Angry shouts rose in response and men chased the donkeys in useless efforts. The soldiers turned to the confusion, at first amused, then concerned. They dashed to chase the donkeys.

"The well, my friend," came a voice from the other side of Thomas. "How long until the soldiers return?"

Thomas turned his head to look into Sir William's grin. Katherine was already halfway across the street to the well.

"How—"

"Misfortune, of course. Who could guess that a rag tied to a donkey's tail might brush against a lamp's flame?"

"Who indeed?" Thomas grinned in return.

The hubbub from the street grew. The smash of glass and roars of rage rose above the clamor.

"Addon," Thomas said, "two gold pieces for your trouble."

Thomas began to search for words to dismiss the young boy, but had no chance to speak. Addon was already backing away, his fingers firmly clasped over the gold.

"The market," Addon blurted. "In this confusion, I can fill my pockets!"

Thomas decided it was not the moment to point out that there was no honor in theft. He sprinted to join Katherine and Sir William at the edge of the well.

3

Thomas squeezed his eyes shut and concentrated on small mercies. *With the deep unknown below, he at least worried little about the soldiers.*

There was a heavy rope attached to a pole at the side of the well. The rope hung at the side of the well and disappeared into the black hole; hundreds of years of friction of rope against stone had worn the edges of the well smooth. The well itself was wide—toe to outstretched fingertips; Thomas could not have reached across.

"If the well does not lead to safety?" Thomas asked.

"What choice?" Sir William countered. "Gates sealed, city walls guarded, and in all probability, a reward offered for our heads. We cannot hide among these people."

Katherine said nothing. She hastily tore the veil from her face and crammed it into a compartment of her cloak. She smiled once at Thomas, then without hesitation, took the rope in her hands, and lowered herself over the edge.

"What choice? Her action is answer enough," Thomas said.

He too wrapped his fingers around the rough hemp of the rope and rolled over the edge. Sir William waited until Thomas had disappeared into the darkness, then followed.

Despite their conversation, less than half a minute had passed from the time of reaching the well to when all three were clinging to the rope and lowering themselves hand over hand. No commands or soldiers' shouts reached them—no one had seen them escape.

Thomas breathed a small prayer of gratitude. They were now safe from detection. Then he prayed they would survive the descent and that the shaft did indeed lead outside the city walls.

For the first ten feet of the descent, they found themselves pushing away from the sides of the well. Then, without warning, the walls seemed to fall away, and it wasn't until Thomas had lowered himself another ten feet, did he understand. Looking upward against the light of the sky as backdrop, he saw that the well shaft actually widened as it deepened.

The sight gave him a prickle of hope. Would not a city as ancient as this slowly build over the well through the centuries? Did this widening of the shaft mean that perhaps there would be room to stand around the pool at its bottom?

It gave him enough hope to ignore the burning in the muscles of his lower arms.

"Thomas!"

"Yes, Sir William," he grunted. It took great effort to breathe normally, let alone speak.

"At the side of this wall. Rungs!"

Thomas grinned relief. The knight had spoken true. A ladder of horizontal iron bars was imbedded into the stone walls of the shaft. *At one time, this well had been meant for more than rope and bucket.*

The rope began to swing.

"Katherine!" Thomas yelped. "This is no time for play!"

"If we . . . reach the . . . rungs," she said, "no person above . . . who seeks to . . . draw water . . . will pull against . . . our weight."

It was dangerous, to be swaying at this dizzying speed an unknown distance from the bottom, but Thomas knew Katherine's logic was correct.

He began to sway in unison.

Moments later, Sir William managed to grasp a rung. He steadied the rope for Thomas and Katherine. Then Sir William yanked hard to test the iron bar. It did not move.

"Dare we hope this fortune holds?" he asked. He did not wait for a reply but released the rope.

Katherine had reached a lower rung. She too relinquished the rope and began to climb downward.

With Sir William's feet about to step onto Thomas' head, there was no choice. Thomas took the rung in front of him and began to feel below for another that would hold the weight of his own feet.

It took less than five minutes to reach the ground—which indeed was a small beach circling the pool of water. And after that—through a cool and dank passageway so low they had to walk bent forward like waddling geese—it took another five minutes to reach a pile of rubble which blocked further movement. Yet from the first moment inside the passage that led away from the wide pool at the bottom of the well shaft, Thomas knew it was the most joyful walk that he had undertaken. Step by cramped step, he felt like singing because of the distant white light that grew larger as they approached. Sunlight. Sunlight and the sound of birds.

They stopped at the rubble that blocked them.

Thomas fell forward and kissed the rocks, which brought forth laughter from Katherine. Sir William caught his enthusiasm and clenched his fist in a victory salute.

"The gamble reaped great profit!" Thomas said when he stood again. "I'll not mind shredding my hands to clear these rocks, for outside are the hills and mountains."

Thomas went to the top of the pile of rubble and threw some rocks backward. The opening at the top increased only slightly.

"No, it's—"

"Not another—"

Sir William and Katherine stopped themselves, for they had begun to berate Thomas in the same breath.

The result was the same. Thomas stopped.

Sir William bowed gravely. "After you, m'lady," he said to Katherine.

Katherine smiled. Thomas knew he would never tire of watching that gentle smile.

"I was about to say," Katherine began, "*No, it's* time I received an explanation."

"Explanation?" Thomas asked.

She nodded. "We were about to leave the city. Until Sir William turned back, and whispered for me to follow. Then he lit the tails of those donkeys, and told me to descend the well. For all I knew, you had both taken leave of your senses."

"Yet you descended," Thomas marveled. "Without protest."

She turned grave eyes upon him. "What is trust untried? Sir William I have always trusted. And only now, in Jerusalem, have I pledged trust to you. With trust, there is acceptance. So I obeyed."

She spread her hands. "But now. . . ."

"Gihon Spring," Thomas explained. "Sir William reminded me of another battle fought in Jerusalem. King David himself, those hundreds upon hundreds of years ago, won this city by sending men up the shaft of the Gihon Spring."

"You did not know for certain the passage still remained," Katherine said.

"No, but we had little choice. And we were led to the most ancient well in Jerusalem."

Katherine nodded slow agreement, then reached upward for Thomas to help her to the top of the pile of rubble.

"Not another stone, please," Sir William said. "That is what *I* had been about to say."

"We cannot remain here," Thomas said.

"Of course not. Yet why should we expose ourselves in the light of day to flee in the heat? Tonight, while the city sleeps, we shall depart from here. By morning, we will be far enough away to purchase horses, perhaps in Bethlehem."

Sir William turned his hands so that his palms were face up. "Feel this air. Cool and comfortable. We can rest here in safety and sleep until nightfall." He flashed a grin from a dirt-smudged face. "The treasure we seek has lain undiscovered for nearly 13 centuries. One day more matters little, does it not?"

4

By midnight they had cleared enough rubble to crawl through to escape. Behind them stood the eastern city walls. Outlined against the moonlight were the silhouettes of sentry soldiers atop those walls. Although the soldiers were barely in crossbow range, Thomas and Katherine and Sir William stayed low and crept from tree to tree as they moved directly away from the city; the moonlight was strong enough to cast shadows, and detection of their presence was too much of a possibility.

Thomas hardly dared whisper until long after they had straightened and begun to walk in long hurried strides.

"Water?" he croaked.

"None," Sir William replied. "And I share your thirst. It seemed as if we moved a mountain!"

They were now among a grove of olive trees, widely spaced in the dry soil. The leaves glittered silver from the moon, and the hills beyond were solid black against the sky and stars and scattered ghostly clouds.

"Thirst . . ." Katherine said. "I would give a king's ransom to dive into a pool. Does the scroll I carry have locations of springs nearby?"

Thomas pictured in his mind the maps he had pored over with scholars in Jerusalem. "We must turn south," he finally said, "cross the plains and then into the hills of Bethlehem. That will be our nearest water. It is a journey that will last until dawn."

"Horses too we shall seek there," Sir William said. "Until now, we have ridden donkeys. While it would be prudent to continue to appear as common travelers, we must cast caution aside. Speed is of the utmost importance."

"Yet horses tire more easily," Katherine countered. "Speed matters little if it cannot be sustained under pursuit."

A slight breeze swirled, so that the shadows of the trees swayed and bounced patterns of dancers across the hard-packed ground.

"Gold is one thing we do have," Thomas mused. "Could we not purchase three or four horses each, so that when one becomes tired of the weight of its rider, we saddle another?"

Sir William clapped Thomas on his right shoulder. "Superb, my friend. We could be on a ship for England within the month."

And then? Thomas smiled at the knight in return, but already was lost in thought. *What might happen in England?* There were only the three of them.

But no. . . .

There was a fourth.

The words again rose in his mind, the words which had haunted Thomas all these months, the first words Sir William had spoken upon their reunion here in the Holy Land.

"That you are here speaks volumes of the dire trouble that faces Magnus," Sir William had said.

Thomas had nodded. Nothing could have prepared him for the words he heard next.

"Yet in this dark cloud exists more than a tiny part of joy." The knight had paused and studied Thomas' face. "For one man has waited many years in exile to see you."

"Yes?" Thomas had asked.

"Your father," had been the astounding reply.

Because of that, Thomas had journeyed through the Holy Land with hope. Indeed, he had learned the truth behind his childhood, finally learned that these two with him could be trusted in a cause that united them, and learned he could trust too the love for Katherine which filled him with peace and joy.

But Sir William had yet to tell him of his father. They had hours of travel ahead, travel in the isolation of night. Thomas would be glad to fill those hours with conversation. And with questions.

They slipped among the shadows, using the receding outline of the city of Jerusalem high upon its hill to give them their bearings as they moved south. Thomas waited several minutes, then spoke again.

"Sir William," he began, "yesterday you informed me of a self-evident truth. Lord Baldwin was not—as he claimed—my father."

"Lord Baldwin." Sir William spat. "He hid among the Merlins for years, claiming to be one of us. Were it not for your test as he tried to deceive you too, we might never have known."

Katherine slipped beside Thomas as they walked. Without speaking, she took his hand, and intertwined her fingers among his. The simplicity of her gesture—a quiet gift of love as they descended as fugitives through the hillside fields—touched him so deeply that his throat tightened. He did not trust himself to speak.

Sir William repeated himself. "Thomas, did you not hear me? You have solved one mystery. It was Lord Baldwin—the traitor among us—and Waleran who were responsible for the fall of Magnus before your birth, the fall that sent all of us into exile here in the Holy Land."

Thomas nodded. Katherine squeezed his hand, a slight pressure of her awareness of how she affected him.

"But my father . . ." Thomas finally found his voice. "Who is my father if not Lord Baldwin?"

"What was that?" Sir William said sharply.

"Who is my—"

"No. I thought I heard movement."

They froze. Thomas and Sir William placed their right hands upon the hilts of their swords—instantly ready for fight. Yet only shadows shifted and teased their eyes, only the sigh of the breeze greeted them.

Sir William relaxed. He began to walk forward again.

This time, Thomas sought Katerhine's hand. He caught a gleam of her teeth in the light of the moon as she smiled.

"Who is your father?" Sir William asked. "Tell me first what you know of your childhood and the Merlins, then I shall reveal what of the rest he has permitted me."

5

"I am a Merlin," Thomas said. Quiet satisfaction filled his voice to call himself such. "I was raised as an orphan in an obscure monastery, near the kingdom of Magnus, which once belonged to us. The nurse who trained me—Sarah—I now know was my mother. She taught me the ways of Merlins, the use of logic and knowledge to fight our battles against the Druids."

"Yes," Katherine whispered. "You *are* a Merlin. For so long we could not trust you. Sarah's death. . . ."

"My *mother's* death," Thomas said firmly. "I was not able to know her as such during her life. Please let me have that now."

Katherine lifted his hand and brushed her lips against the backs of his fingers in apology.

As Thomas continued, he noted that the knight did not cease in his vigil of the shadows which surrounded them. Their conversation continued as they walked.

"My mother died before I was old enough to be told of

Merlins and Druids and their age-old battle," Thomas said. "I set out to conquer Magnus with the knowledge I had been given, unaware of the hidden Druid masters of that castle and kingdom. And for the last year I have felt as a pawn between both the Druids and Merlins in their unseen battle."

Sir William stopped. He spun so quickly that his sword banged his leg.

"Thomas, we had no choice."

"I know," Thomas replied, almost weary. "You could not know whether the Druids had discovered me in the monastery and converted me."

"There is more," Katherine said. "More and terrible things. Sir William told me what the Druids truly intend as they expand their power across England."

Sir William began to walk again. Thomas and Katherine followed. "It is a horror that sorrows me to repeat," Sir William said, now moving briskly as if attempting to dispel anger. His dark shadow seemed to flow across the rocky ground in front of them.

"Thomas, you know full well that the Druids have begun to conquer in the most insidious way possible, by posing as Priests of the Holy Grail, proclaiming false miracles to sway all the people."

"Yes," Thomas said. Few memories were closer than those of how he had fled in exile because of the Druid priests.

"This is the same question I asked of Katherine." The knight paused, recalling the words. "Through the sham of false miracles, how long until the Priests of the Holy Grail convince town after town to abandon one religion for another? How long until the priests of the Roman church are powerless?"

Thomas understood instantly. "The entire structure of a country is then threatened! The King of England receives his power only because the people believe he rules by the authority of the Roman church and by the authority of God! If the people no longer believe in that authority, all the noble men and the king will face rebellion!"

"To be replaced by the chosen of the Druid priests," Katherine finished for him. "But there is more at stake."

Now Sir William was clenching his fists, and he walked so quickly that Thomas and Katherine were pressed to stay in stride.

The knight almost hissed his anger. "Thomas, your Merlin education and training has given you the history of mankind. You know that 500 years of dark ages have passed, dark ages when knowledge was scarce and all people were held in chains by ignorance. Only now has the light begun to appear. Advances in medicine and science are upon us, and through the written word, are shared from man to man, country to country. Mankind now begins to advance!"

Sir William stopped again, the passion of his words too much to let him walk. "Thomas, I have thought of this so many times that I have the words memorized! Listen to me! It is possible that the day will arrive when fair laws protect every man, when abundance of food and medicine lets a common man live to be forty, yes, even fifty years of age! When it will be common to read, so that all receive the pleasure you and I do from books! When ignorance is dropped and because of it, leaders of men must respond to the will of the people! This day may someday arrive, even if it takes generations after you and I have left this earth. A day when such abundance and ease of living causes nations to exist in peace."

Thomas felt wonder, to see this war-hardened warrior so transformed.

"If the Druids conquer and begin to rule," Sir William said, "they will bar the people from knowledge, for their own power is derived from the ignorance of the people. They will end this slow progress that has been made by the learned men of our country. And these ages of darkness—" he faltered. "These ages of darkness will be upon mankind for centuries more."

"This is the cause we fight," Thomas said, half-filled with joy at understanding the battle, half-filled with dread at the enormity of the stakes.

"Yes," Sir William said. "Merlin himself founded Magnus in the age of King Arthur for this cause—an unseen battle that has raged between Merlins and Druids for eight centuries. And you hold the final secrets to the battle."

"I?"

"Together, when we return to England, this secret can be unlocked, just as surely as we shall find the treasure shown on the scroll which Katherine carries. With both, we will have the chance to overcome the odds."

"Along with my father?"

Before Sir William could replay, shadows detached themselves from beneath the trees to glide and surround them.

The shadows became men, men with drawn curved swords that gleamed in the moonlight.

"Only fools travel at night," came the hoarse whisper. "Fools who pay for their mistakes with blood."

6

The knight reacted without hesitation. He withdrew his sword and lashed outward in a single movement so quickly that two men dropped to clutch their arms with shrieks of agony before any other bandit moved in the darkness.

Then, three men swarmed the knight, swords flashing downward in the moonlight.

Sir William danced tight circles. He struck outward with a fury of steel against steel which sent sparks in all directions and, incredibly, managed to press the attack against all three.

Thomas, almost mesmerized by the skill of the knight's swordplay, nearly paid for that fascination with his life. Had the moon been behind a cloud, he would not have caught the glint of movement at his side. But the silver of the moon saved him, and the shine of steel gave him barely enough warning to dodge backward as a great curved sword slashed downward.

The point of that sword ripped his sleeve, and Thomas spun again, knowing the bandit would strike again soon.

A vicious horizontal swing. Thomas sucked in his stomach, bending forward to pull his lower body away from the arc of the sword. Again, the swish of fabric as his cloak parted to razored steel.

Another vicious swing. This one less close, for Thomas had adjusted to the rough terrain and moved with the nimbleness of desperation.

Another attacker joined.

Thomas ducked, then sprinted to a tree. He struggled to free his own sword but was hampered by his ripped cloak.

Both attackers stayed in pursuit.

Thomas edged around the tree, using it to protect his back as he fought to clear his sword.

Where was Katherine? How many bandits? Was Sir William still alive? Thomas' thoughts scrambled as he did. *We must survive! Duck this sword!*

Thomas felt the pluck of air as the sword whooshed over his head.

There was a thud as the sword bit into the olive tree.

The bandit grunted at the impact and yanked at his sword to pull it free. Thomas took advantage and, while the bandit had both arms extended to grip the sword, kicked upward with all his strength. His foot buried itself in the softness of the bandit's stomach and sent him retching.

No time to relax!

There was another swoosh as the second bandit swung across. His sword bounced off the tree.

And still—Thomas noted grimly—the clank of sword against swords echoed through the night air. *Sir William was alive. Where was Katherine?*

Thomas stepped away from another slash and still fought to clear his own sword. The distraction was a deadly mistake.

For Thomas stumbled.

He recovered with a quick half-step, but the off-balance movement threw his right foot into the arch of a root which curled above the hard ground. He frantically tried to pull free, and a bolt of tearing pain from his ankle forced him to grunt. *Jammed!*

Another frantic pull, despite the pain.

Nothing.

And the curved sword was now raised high. A snarling wolf grin from the bandit as he savored the certain death he was about to inflict upon Thomas.

"Halt!"

Katherine's voice, clear and strong, carried through the trees.

"Halt! Listen to my words!"

The sword above faltered, but did not descend. Farther away, the clank of swords ended.

Thomas flicked his eyes away from the upraised sword and glanced at the bandit's face. It mirrored surprise.

A woman's voice. It has shocked them all into curiosity.

As if proving his guess right, the bandits craned their heads in all directions, trying to locate her voice.

"Here, in the tree," Katherine called. A shifting cloud broke away from the moon, and suddenly her silhouette was easy to see against the light. She stood balanced on a thick branch, far from the ground.

Thomas grinned. *Katherine had found safety during the distraction of Sir William's instant attack.*

His grin died at her next words.

"I promise you far greater treasure than the mere coins we carry! I carry a scroll which leads to great wealth," Katherine called again. Her voice remained easy to hear above the quickening breeze. To confirm her words, she waved the narrow tube of the rolled parchment.

With the attention so focused on Katherine, Thomas considered making a move for his sword. Then decided against it. Katherine had managed to bring a temporary truce. He would trust she had reason to reveal the scroll. Besides, he noted more shadows moving among the trees. There were now at least a dozen bandits, with more joining every minute. Any fight now would most surely be lost.

"We are not fools," the bandit who had first spoken replied as he edged to the tree. "Why should we believe that the scroll leads to treasure?"

"Because we will remain your prisoners until we lead you to this treasure," Katherine said evenly. "Our lives will be payment enough for a lie."

"Yes, I understand," the bandit said. He moved again.

"No!" Katherine said sharply.

"No?" the voice faked hurt surprise.

"No, you will not be able to reach me soon enough to get the scroll," Katherine said. She began to tear the scroll into shreds, an action easy to see in the moonlight. Pieces of the scroll fluttered away with the breeze.

"We carry the knowledge of this treasure in our heads. Now you must let us live."

Long moments of silence followed.

"This is acceptable," the bandit said. "You have made a bargain."

The bandit raised his voice. "Men! Hold your swords!"

Thomas let out a breath that he hadn't realized he'd been holding.

"Yet listen to my words, woman," the bandit finished with silky menace. "Should you not lead us to the treasure, you shall all discover how it feels to die when your skin is peeled slowly from your bodies."

7

"You *do* remember all those marks upon the scroll," Katherine whispered to Thomas. "We *shall* find that treasure. Shall we not?"

"Or die?" Thomas asked with a wry grin. "Last night, I wanted to dance for joy that you had found a way to save our lives. This morning. . . ."

He shrugged to indicate the busy camp around them. Growing sunlight showed evidence of at least twenty men. That shrug brought a wince to his face. Hours earlier, the bandits had savagely bound his hands behind his back with strips of wet leather. Now dry, the leather bit even deeper into his skin.

Katherine interpreted his wince as doubt.

"I had no choice," she said quietly. "Your knowledge was our only hope."

"*Is* our only hope," Thomas corrected her. "And at the very least, you have gained us time—time we did not have last night as the swords clashed."

Thomas did not add that he wondered how little value there was in gained time. Chances of escape seemed impossible. Katherine too was bound, as was Sir William, who sat well guarded on a flat rock on the opposite side of the makeshift camp, which was hidden in a small dusty fold of the hill. Bandits herded them constantly. Indeed, an hour had passed since the gray of dawn and as all prepared to march, this was the first moment Katherine had been able to speak privately with Thomas.

Thomas watched the bandits carefully, gauging their alertness. All of them—lean and wary—moved with fast, certain efficiency as they performed their tasks. *Men who hunted,* Thomas thought. *And who had been hunted. They would not be easy to fool.*

Their own guard was now returning with a bowl of water. Like most of the others, he had a ragged black beard. A short sword was attached to one side of his belt, a scimitar—those heavy curved weapons of destruction—hung from the belt's other side.

Water slopped over the edge of the bowl as the guard approached. Thomas licked his cracked lips as he watched the water soak into the ground.

The guard stopped in front of them. Thomas shook his head at the offered bowl.

"The woman first," Thomas said.

The guard stared, then blinked, then grudgingly smiled. "The woman first," he repeated. "Not only protected by Rashim, but also protected by one with his hands bound."

Katherine leaned forward to drink from the offered bowl. Since her hands were tied behind her back, she had to rely on the guard to tip the bowl as she drank.

Protected by Rashim. The words echoed through Thomas' mind. The leader of the bandits had seen Katherine at dawn's first light and smiled with evil.

"She is not to be harmed in any way," Rashim had said, his face dark as he stood against the light of the sun. He had stroked his beard and smiled coldly. "Not an angel with this beauty."

There had been no threat in his words, but Thomas shivered every time he remembered the threat of his tone.

And now Rashim paced long, unhurried strides toward them again. He wore the long white cloth of a nomad accustomed to endless hours in the heat. The top of his head was covered with a black band across his forehead holding the veils away from his face. His eyes flashed glittering black above a giant hooked nose. The lines around his mouth were etched deep, lines which had long since turned downward from constant snarls.

"This day has already burned long," Rashim said without preamble. "I have readied my men for travel. At this moment, finally, I will listen to you bargain for your lives."

"Last night—" Katherine began to protest.

"Last night only saved you until morning. Convince me first the treasure exists, then we depart. If not—" Rashim paused and shrugged, "the vultures will feast upon your bones."

He stared at Thomas, trying to cow him with a harsh, unblinking gaze.

Thomas stared back, forcing his own eyes to hide all thoughts. They were steady gray eyes which now matched in color and warmth the bleak waters of the North Sea in a November gale. Thomas kept his hair slightly longer than was custom. Tied back, it added strength to the impression immediately given through square shoulders, a high, intelligent forehead and a straight noble nose. It was a quiet strength of confidence; Rashim could not know, of course, that Thomas had spent the entire previous winter in the English kingdom of Magnus, learning and practicing swordplay. The hall outside had rung again and again each day with the clang of steel against steel. No man could handle a broadsword for hour after hour without developing considerable bulk, a bulk shown in his corded, muscular arms now bound so uncomfortably behind a wide chest.

"Tell me the story," Rashim commanded.

Thomas began, in a low and calm voice, to explain, "The story begins 1,600 years ago—"

"Impossible!" Rashim exploded.

"Sixteen hundred years ago," Thomas continued as if he had not been interrupted, "in the land from whence we came. Britain. Then, before the Romans conquered, Druids ruled the land. They knew secrets of science and astronomy and kept their power through secrecy."

Rashim's eyes narrowed in concentration.

Thomas did not change the levelness of his voice. "When the Romans conquered, much as did the Romans who ruled this land in the time of Christ . . ."

Now Rashim nodded at the facts which he already knew.

" . . . the Druid leaders in Britain formed a hidden circle within society, a hidden circle with great wealth. Later, a Roman general discovered this Druid circle. The general, Julius Severus, who ruled Britain some hundred years after the death of Christ, did not expose what he knew of the Druids and their accumulated gold. To let Rome know of the Druids would also let Rome know of their wealth and almost magical powers. Instead, Severus plundered the Druids in one fell swoop, taking a great fortune in gold."

Thomas did not add the rest of what he knew, that Julius Severus also managed to find and keep the book of the most valued Druid secrets of potions and deception. A book to stagger the imagination with the power it might yield its owner.

"You have my interest," Rashim admitted. "But the story is centuries old, and in a land halfway across the world." Rashim took a dagger from his belt and with its tip, and as a casual threat, began to pick dirt from beneath his fingernails. "How did such a treasure—as you claim—come to be hidden here?"

"You searched us," Thomas replied. "In my possession you found a small, tightly bound book of parchment."

Rashim nodded, almost impatient for proof of a great treasure.

"That book contains the notes of many who searched through the centuries for clues to the treasure. It is meant to assist any who held the scroll which Katherine destroyed last night. Without the scrolled map, this book is useless."

"A book in your possession because . . ."

"That story is long and tedious." Thomas affected a sigh of weariness, hoping Rashim would not press him. It was not the time to reveal the Merlins, or their age-old battle against Druids. It was not the time to reveal that the small book had continued directions to the monastery in Jerusalem where Thomas had sought the scholars who would help him continue his search.

"Then make me believe that the gold did reach this land," Rashim demanded. The dagger was now clenched in his fist. "Force me to believe why it might still be hidden."

"The Roman general was summoned from Britain to quell a revolt of the Jews, here in the Holy Land. Severus could not trust his treasure to be left behind, so he arranged to take it with him. Once here, he and his Roman soldiers destroyed nearly a thousand Jewish villages, and a half million were slain. The Jewish rebels were finally defeated in their last refuge—caves in the Judean desert, near the Dead Sea."

Rashim's eyes flashed greed. "The caves of refuge! We all know of those," he said. "But I have always discounted them as myth, for stories were told of entire families living for months inside the earth."

"The General Severus was recalled to Rome almost immediately after his victory in the Holy Land," Thomas replied with an unfriendly nod of agreement. "The treasure he had taken with him from Britain, he could not take to Rome, for discovery of it by Roman officials would mean his death. And shortly after arriving in Rome, he died of sudden illness, taking his secret to the grave."

"Why the caves?" Rashim persisted. "In this entire land, why are you certain the treasure lies in the caves?"

Thomas closed his eyes and recited what he recalled from the letter of a man now dead. "During one skirmish against the Jews near these caves, General Julius Severus lost 20 men in battle—against a handful of unarmed rebels. These 20 men, Severus reported, died as a portion of the cave collapsed upon them, and their bodies could not be recovered. Is it not more likely that these would be the 20 men who transported the treasure? Is it not likely that the surest way for Julius Severus to guard his secret would be to kill those 20, in the cave where the treasure was buried?"

"Ahah," Rashim purred.

Thomas nodded.

Before Rashim could speak next, a bandit, almost exhausted, ran into camp and called for him. Rashim hurried away, and spent several minutes with his head bent low, listening to the man. Several times Rashim glanced back at Thomas and Katherine. Then he spun and returned.

For a moment, he did not speak. He only stared downward at Thomas.

Without warning, Rashim lashed out with his open hand and slapped Thomas across the side of his head.

"You have deceived us!"

Thomas tasted warm wet salt. Blood. He refused to lick it away from the corner of his mouth as it began to dribble into tiny spots onto the rocks at his feet.

Another wild lash.

Thomas stared back. He concentrated on the pain, knowing that to think of anything else would weaken his resolve not to show response.

"You have deceived us!" Rashim repeated again. He raised his hand again, but Thomas did not flinch.

Rashim dropped his hand without striking.

Had he decided Thomas could not be intimidated?

He studied Thomas. In return, Thomas studied him.

There were long moments of silence, broken only by the buzzing of nearby flies. An idle part of Thomas' mind noted the flies were swarming around the blood at his feet.

"You told us of treasure," Rashim thundered. "But you did not tell us of soldiers!"

"Neither did we tell you of the ocean. Or of mountains. Or of birds. Or of anything else that exists in this world. What significance is there in soldiers?" It took effort for Thomas not to mumble.

Rashim half closed his eyes, as if exerting great control over his rage. He opened them again. "One is not followed by the ocean. Nor by mountains. And the birds which follow you may soon not have far to go. For they shall be vultures circling your dead body."

Rashim pointed past Thomas. "I have been told that soldiers have followed your tracks away from Jerusalem. That they are nearly within sight of these hills. Barely an hour away."

"We did not know," Thomas said. "And it does not change the matter of the wealth promised last night. Moreover, if I am dead or my friends harmed, the treasure will not be yours."

Men scurried in all directions as they loaded donkeys.

"Indeed, indeed." Rashim's smile caressed Thomas with cruelty. "Fortunately for you, the soldiers' pursuit readily confirms there is truth in your story."

Rashim lashed out one final time, hitting Thomas with such force that it loosened several of his teeth.

"Take care we don't leave you behind to be crucified," Rashim said.

"His death means you forfeit the treasure," Katherine said quietly. "He is the only one of us who studied the scroll."

Rashim laughed. "Perhaps there is different treasure to be had."

He laughed again. "Your hand in marriage," Rashim said as he bowed to Katherine, "might well be worth the forfeit, even if an angel like you might spend our first months together mourning Thomas' early death."

8

On the morning of the third day of slow travel toward the Dead Sea, Thomas almost wished instead that Rashim had removed his skin in small strips as threatened.

They had left the rugged hills near Jerusalem, traveled through valleys filled with fields and olive trees for only a short distance more, then abruptly reached great and desolate ravines carved through steep ridges of sandstone and limestone.

It was difficult enough to stumble ahead with his hands bound behind his back. The pressing heat squeezed sweat from every pore, sweat that immediately turned to tiny balls of mud from the choking dust. Despite the pain on the inside of his mouth, Thomas refused to ask for water, and it was rarely given.

The bandits' path took them through twists and turns and difficult climbs and descents as they followed the course of the ravines. The bandits were hampered by their lack of knowledge of this forbidding terrain, and they could not race forward and risk trapping themselves in a ravine with no exit. Instead, scouts had been sent ahead in various directions to report back the safest routes. They moved so slowly that it had taken them two full days to cover a mere 25 miles; on each of the two nights—because of pursuit by the Mameluke soldiers—the bandits had set up camp without daring to seek the comfort of fires.

Thus far, the bandits had made no efforts to cover their tracks. To do so properly would have taken too much time, a luxury they did not have with over 100 soldiers—as reported, advancing steadily behind them—at an equally slow pace. The soldiers lagged because of the bulk of their numbers as well as the heat which worsened with each step closer to the bottom of the massive rift which held the Dead Sea, some 1,300 feet below sea level.

Now, early in the morning of the third day, the heat was already oppressive and progress was still slow. The bandits hugged the base of cliffs so tall on each side of the narrow valley that Thomas had to crane his head backward to see where the rugged edges met the sky. Ahead, where the valley broke to open horizon, was their destination: the Dead Sea.

Thomas wished he could speak with Katherine. Or with Sir William. But Rashim kept them well separated to prevent them from planning escape.

Thomas despaired. Hands bound, stripped of everything but his clothes, without water, and exhausted from heat and pain, his chances seemed hopeless. He knew the same applied to Sir William. While Katherine's hands had been unbound—Rashim treated her more gently—she too had nothing that would help them in a fight or in escape.

And they could not leave without the priceless books which had been taken from the Druids so many centuries earlier. Even if escape were possible now, they could not turn back.

Thomas reviewed what must lie ahead.

In Jerusalem, near the ruins of the temple—destroyed by the Romans 1,200 years earlier—Thomas had visited a monastery which survived from the days of the Crusades. The scholars inside, allowed to live by the grace of the Mamelukes, were shy and elderly, with flowing white beards that touched their chests when they sat. They had not been surprised to see Thomas, nor the small book with its directions to their monastery. When Thomas had asked of the Cave of Letters and the Dead Sea, two of the scholars had stood immediately and retrieved ancient scrolls from nearby chambers. They had retraced the markings onto another, smaller scroll, and accepted quietly the gold offered by Thomas.

When you reach the Dead Sea, go south, the scholars had told him as they ran old, thin fingers across the scroll. *It is a land so bleak you will discover no towns on the edge of the shores. You will easily find the ruins of Engedi, for there are no other ruins, and this one is marked clearly by the dozens of collapsed stone buildings. The Dead Sea will be on your left and deep ravines on your right. Do not enter the ravine that leads from the hills into Engedi, but travel farther. Do not enter the next ravine, nor the next. The fourth ravine will lead you to the caves of Bar Kokhba, where he and the last Jewish rebels had died. Why is it you want to know, young one? How is it that you even have the knowledge to ask of a rebel so obscure?*

As he walked each painful step across the scorching earth, and despite his despair, Thomas smiled to remember the unforceful curiosity which had shone from the luminous eyes of the Jerusalem scholars as they posed him those final questions. Grateful that the Mamelukes found their work both harmless and useful, the scholars had no concern for politics, no concern for wealth, only for learning.

From an old one such as yourselves, Thomas had answered. *One who would have loved to spend endless hours pouring through these scrolls with you.*

They had smiled mysteriously in return and nodded as Thomas left them in the quiet chambers of study.

"What cause have you to smile?" demanded Rashim.

In his thoughts, Thomas had not noticed the attention of the bandit leader.

"I think merely of the treasure which will buy our lives," Thomas replied after a moment, for he had been so engrossed in recollection that it was not easy to dispell the yearnful feeling that he was not still in the dark cool chambers of the Jerusalem monastery. "You will fulfill your end of the bargain, will you not? You will release us after we have led you to the wealth?"

"You have my word of honor," Rashim said.

They both knew the words were lies.

At that moment, anger surged inside Thomas with the suddenness of fire exploding from dry bush. *This man with the taunting smile of evil meant to take from him his life, and far worse, perhaps take Katherine.*

The anger so completely replaced his despair that Thomas forgot his helplessness, forgot that he had no weapons, no means of using any Merlin scientific secrets. Somehow, and he did not know how, Rashim would be defeated.

Long after Rashim walked away, the anger burned within Thomas, then became cold determination. Thomas would keep his life and return to England with Katherine and the knight.

A shout rose at the first sight of the water of the Dead Sea.

Thomas gritted his teeth. The Dead Sea. It meant he had until nightfall to find a way to live.

9

"I have heard much of this sea," Rashim said, gesturing past the wide beach. "Were not the soldiers in pursuit, I would send one of my men to test its waters."

Thomas concentrated on his balance. It was difficult work to slog through the sand along its shore. Without freely swinging hands, the task was doubly difficult.

"Yes," Rashim was saying. "I am told the water is so salty that men float in it like pieces of wood."

Just one more step, Thomas told himself, *one more step. And then another. We have traveled beyond Engedi. The next valley is the one which holds the Cave of Letters. Just one more step.*

Rashim grabbed Thomas by the arm as he stumbled.

"My friend," he said with a wide, false smile, "we cannot have you die."

Rashim whistled for a bandit somewhere behind them.

Thomas was too exhausted to lift his head.

The bandit ran close, and Rashim impatiently called for water.

Within moments, Thomas was drinking deeply. He did not mind the musky leather-skin taste of water hot from hours in the sun.

Rashim pulled the water bag away.

"Are we near our destination?" Rashim asked.

Thomas closed his eyes.

Rashim slapped him. Gently.

Thomas opened his eyes. He was able to briefly focus again.

Beyond Rashim, lay the beach that led to the flat, waveless water of the Dead Sea. Its waters appeared ghost white from the glare of the sun. Wavering in the heat, yet somehow appearing close enough to touch, were the high hills on the opposite side of the sea, hardly more than ten miles away.

"Are we near our destination?" Rashim repeated. "Already we can see the dust of the soldiers behind us. Their pace quickens now that they too have reached the shoreline."

Thomas nodded in a delirium of confusion. All he wanted to do was lie in shade, close his eyes, and, if it were his time, finally die. His mouth had swollen and cracked from the blows dealt by Rashim earlier. His feet were blistered, his arms, numb. Because his hands were bound so tightly, each jolting step had seemed to pull his arms from his sockets.

"Where?" Rashim was saying. "Where from here?"

Thomas tried to mumble something. It was not soon enough or clear enough for Rashim's liking.

"Bring the girl," Rashim commanded the bandit who had brought water.

When Thomas opened his eyes again to sway where he stood, Katherine was there, in front of him.

It felt like a dream, like all he had to do was push aside the curtains of white haze between them and he could reach out and touch her.

But his arms wouldn't move.

A sharp crack brought him back instantly.

Rashim's hand had flashed to strike Katherine flat across her face. A red welt appeared, showing clearly the outlines of Rashim's fingers and hand.

Rage took Thomas again, brought to him final reserves of strength. He set his feet wider, and the swaying stopped.

"Where from here?" Rashim asked again and raised his hand to strike Katherine once more.

Rage crystallized the thoughts which tumbled through Thomas' mind. One thought took hold and grew with his rage. A thought of hope.

"Send most of your men ahead," Thomas said firmly. "They must continue along the shoreline."

"Now you give commands?" Rashim asked.

"The soldiers," Thomas said. *This small chance may be all we will be given. I must convince him.*

"Soldiers?"

"Surely if all of us turn away from the sea into the valley of the caves, the soldiers will follow. And the valley has no exit. We will all be trapped."

Rashim squinted as he considered the advice.

"We will send most ahead to draw the soldiers," Rashim finally agreed. "And cover our own tracks as we go into the valley."

"Yes," Thomas said. "But Katherine and the knight must go with us."

Thomas held his breath. *What little chance they had could only occur if the bandits were divided. If Katherine or the knight continued on with the others. . . .*

Rashim shrugged.

Thomas then felt his stomach shrink with momentary fear to the hardness and size of a walnut. *He agrees easily because he cares little what happens to us when the treasure is found.*

"As you say, the girl and the knight travel with us," Rashim said with a mock bow. "After all, I am a man who bargains fairly."

Thomas took a deep breath and looked around. Hands bound, he had no other way to point except with a jerk of his head in the direction of the rocky ravine just ahead. In his mind, the directions echoed clearly. *The fourth ravine will lead you to the caves of Bar Kokhba, where the last Jewish rebels had died. There are five caves high on the sandstone walls. Bar Kokhba took his last stand in the fifth cave, the one farthest west from the Dead Sea.*

Thomas prayed it would not be the cave where he and the knight would join those rebels in the slumber of death.

One hour later, he and the knight and Katherine, along with Rashim and five of the largest bandits, stood at the top of a path, near the dark circle of a cave's entrance.

10

"My good friend," Rashim said. "I am pleased to discover you did not deceive us about the caves. Perhaps now it is time for you to die."

Rashim nodded once.

The largest of the bandits drew a scimitar high above Thomas' head and waited for another nod.

Thomas set his jaw straight and stared straight ahead.

I have done everything I can, Thomas thought. *If this is how it must end, it is the Lord's will. I will not beg or show fear.*

The sword hung against the sky.

Thomas became vividly aware of sharp details—the spider which darted across a nearby boulder, the intricate shadows of the spiked leaves of brush surrounding the cave's entrance, the scream of the hawk overhead.

In that long, timeless heartbeat, Thomas became overwhelmed by awe. And joy. *The smallest of things reflect eternity,* he thought, suddenly unaware of the sword. What a marvel, that a creature as insignificant as a spider may be constructed so perfectly that it moves with such grace on legs lighter than thread. What an incredible mystery, the forces which direct this bush to grow, to shoot forth branches and leaves. What a wonder, the hawk which learns to conquer even the wind, and untamed, goes where no man might predict.

The passage of a moment became meaningless. The peace within him expanded and rushed outward, as if Thomas himself were becoming a part of the spider, of the bush, of the hawk.

My God, he thought, *You are Master of all of this. How can I fear death?*

"No!" a voice reached Thomas. "Do not kill him yet."

Thomas blinked.

The pain of his swollen mouth returned. The throbbing of his blistered feet, the ache of his arms. No longer did it seem he could hear a spider's steps across the boulder, no longer did it seem he rode the wind on the shoulder of a hawk.

"Do not kill him *yet?*" Rashim said. "Yet?"

Katherine nodded.

"My decision is to be with you, Rashim. Alive," she replied. "Let Thomas die as he retrieves the treasure."

Rashim stroked his chin.

"You intrigue me. Tell me more."

"Have the sword lowered," Katherine said.

Rashim nodded at the bandit, and the sword dropped from the sky.

"What if this is not the right cave?" Katherine asked. "Do we have time to search all the others? Will the soldiers remain in pursuit of the others indefinitely?"

Rashim pursed his lips together, not fully convinced.

"And there remains this cave," she said. "If you and I are to share the treasure, I wish to see *you* unharmed. Send

Thomas ahead. Let him be inflicted by vipers. Let him stumble into bottomless pits. Let him risk his life for us. If I am to be wedded to you, I wish to live in luxury."

Thomas stared at the ground. He told himself that she again was bargaining for time, forestalling as long as possible the moment of their deaths, hoping against all hopes that something might occur to set them free.

But enough truth rang from her voice for him to feel the gnawing of doubt, and he realized he would rather have died then, than discover betrayal by her inside the cave.

Rashim thought for only a few seconds.

"Find brush for torches," he directed his men. "We shall let the knight and his friend direct our way."

He grabbed Katherine by the arm and pinched cruelly. "This one remains with me as we follow. Should she—or they—falter, I will slice her throat in two."

Thomas and Sir William stood side by side, ten paces ahead of Rashim and Katherine and the five other bandits.

"The strength of your arm?" Sir William whispered.

"I can barely hold this torch," Thomas replied. His fingers were still numb, even though the bonds had been cut fifteen minutes earlier.

"Begin!" shouted Rashim. His voice now reflected nervousness. This was a man accustomed to ruling other men, not searching for the tomb of long-dead Roman soldiers.

Rashim's command still echoed as Thomas and Sir William moved ahead. The cave roof was beyond the reach of the flames of the torch, and the light that licked into all corners cast yellow fingers and gray shadows which made it difficult to judge the depths of the passage.

"Tell me when your strength has returned," Sir William whispered as they shuffled ahead.

Only a part of Thomas' mind heard. Another part was repeating Katherine's words. *Vipers and bottomless pits. What was ahead of them?*

Thomas focused on the ground immediately in front. Their light was not strong enough to illuminate much beyond them, and to search the far shadows played too many tricks with his imagination.

"Tell me when your strength has returned," Sir William whispered again.

"We cannot attack," Thomas countered with equal softness. "He holds a knife to Katherine's throat. And we have no weapons."

"Where we find treasure, we will find the remains of soldiers," Sir William said. "Where we find those soldiers, we will find their weapons."

Yes! The knight was correct. *It increased their odds, no matter how slim!* Thomas grinned into the darkness ahead. And immediately regretted it. His lips cracked again and he tasted his own blood.

His mind now raced. *We have succeeded in dividing this small army of bandits. Our hands are now free. We may have weapons soon. But how to get Katherine from the knife at her throat?*

Another thought. *Will the sight of treasure prove to be enough of a distraction? Will that give the knight the final edge he needs?*

The cave tunnel widened suddenly into a hall.

Light gleamed off something metal at the far corner of their vision.

"How much farther?" demanded Rashim. Thomas could hear Rashim's quickened breathing. *This fear will be to our advantage as well.*

"I cannot say," Thomas called back. "But look here. Signs

of those who lived in this cave!"

The gleam of light off bronze became a wide rounded bowl, and intricately designed pitchers.

"Keep your distance," Rashim warned.

Thomas and Sir William moved ahead.

Behind them, they heard the clang of metal against metal as one of the bandits prodded the vessels with a sword.

The hall narrowed again, became one passage and then almost immediately divided into two.

"Which side?" the knight asked.

"Does it matter?" Thomas said. "This entire cave must be explored."

Thomas dared not voice his single biggest fear . . . *that the treasure already be plundered. Obscure and remote as this cave was, what if another over the centuries had solved the riddle?*

What if—

Thomas sucked in a breath.

Intent on watching the ground for snakes, he noticed something the knight had missed.

A footprint.

Then he relaxed.

In this still air, a footprint would be preserved for centuries.

The tunnel widened again, and looking back at the torches of the bandits, Thomas could see that the other passage, the one they had chosen to ignore, had rejoined them again.

What was ahead?

They moved into another hall. Discovered a basket of skulls, a tangled fishing net, and a large basin scooped into a wall.

"Water reservoir," Sir William whispered. "Dozens of people may have lived in this cave!"

"Move quickly!" Rashim called.

Thomas hoped Rashim's knife would not tremble against Katherine's throat with the nervousness now so obvious in his voice.

Farther on, they found a bundle of letters, the edges of the parchment so well preserved that Thomas relaxed. This parchment has withstood the centuries; a footprint, too, would do the same.

The hall ended abruptly.

Thomas and the knight carefully searched for another passage, but found none.

"We return," Thomas announced to the bandits who still followed ten paces behind. "There is one other passage to explore. One where this hall began."

The bandits gave them ample room to move by. *Despite the threat of a knife at Katherine's throat,* Thomas realized, *despite the weapons they held, they still fear the knight's fighting ability.*

The realization gave him even more hope.

Now, we must find the treasure. And the Druid book.

Twenty steps down the other passage, they did.

11

Thomas and Sir William held their torches out over the pit. The light did not extend downward enough to show bottom, nor the other side.

"What is it?" Rashim asked from behind them. "Why do you stop? What do you see?"

"Only darkness," the knight replied. "The darkness of a great pit."

Thomas lifted his light to survey the nearby cave floor. At the edge of the light, he saw a ladder made of rope. He retrieved it, and lifted it partway to his waist, so that Rashim could see it too.

"The treasure lies below," Thomas said with a confidence he did not feel. *Why else would a ladder have been left nearby?*

"Hurry then," Rashim said. "Bring me a sample."

Thomas knew he must continue to act the role of one helpless with the fear of death. It was an easy role to play.

"But you will only kill me once the treasure has been proven."

"Better than a slow death," Rashim said. From behind the torch light, his fierce face was filled with shadows.

Thomas bowed his head, as if he had been beaten. Then he noticed a small line of dark powder that followed around the edge of the pit.

He dropped the ladder, fell to his knees to retrieve it, and managed to smear some of the powder on his fingers.

Strange, he thought as he turned his back and touched the powder lightly with his tongue. *This bitterness has a familiar taste. And why a line that surrounds the pit as far as I can see?*

He had no time to ponder further.

Two of the bandits were at his side, holding their hands out to grasp the rope ladder. They lowered it over the side.

Another bandit prodded Thomas with the point of his sword.

With pretended reluctance, Thomas began to climb downward. The bandits were so large, and held the rope so steady, that the ladder hardly moved at all with his full weight upon it.

Thomas took one final look upward to mark Sir William's position. *If I find swords below, I cannot falter upon my return. I must toss him one without hesitation.*

Sir William's strong face regarded him without changing expression. Then a slow wink, and Thomas felt strengthened.

Thomas lowered himself slowly, one hand holding the side of the rope ladder, another the torch.

How far down?

He counted twenty-five steps, then touched bottom.

"What do you see?" Rashim called down.

Thomas realized that from Rashim's position, there would only be the glare of the torchlight. No one on the edge above would be able to see below the torch, see what Thomas now beheld.

There were piles of large leather bags stacked along one of the smooth vertical walls of the pit. The bags bulged as if filled with stones.

Gold?

Thomas moved sideways, still carrying the torch high so that the glare of the light shielded the observers above.

He kicked at one the bags. The leather, dried from centuries of cool air, broke open. Chunks of gold trinkets and scattered jewels fell on the floor.

"What is it?" Rashim called again.

Thomas did not reply. He cared little for the treasure, glad only that it could be used as a distraction.

He needed to find swords.

Thomas moved again, roving around the bottom of the pit. And nearly stumbled over a skeleton. Patches of clothing and armor covered it. It lay in a curled position, as if the soldier had fallen asleep, never to wake again.

The torch light flickered over another skeleton. Then another. All in the same positions.

Horror hit Thomas with the realization of how these soldiers had died.

Someone above had taken their ladder away.

It made too much sense. They would have carried the treasure down, then been abandoned so that the secret of the treasure's location would die with them.

"What have you found?" Rashim was saying, breaking into Thomas' spell of horror.

"The price of greed," Thomas said in a choked voice.

He pushed beyond the terrible sight. *There—stacked neatly against the wall—swords.*

Thomas took two, and tucked them into the belt beneath his cloak. He hurried back to the leather bags, and took a handful of jewels.

Then he dropped the torch and stamped the flame into extinction.

To rise out of the darkness will give an advantage . . .

"What goes there?" Frustration was evident in Rashim's voice.

"Treasure!" Thomas tried to inject excitement into his voice. It was difficult. He could only hate the impulse that had driven men to let others die in this way. And for only the coldness of gold.

"Treasure!" Thomas repeated. "I cannot carry both the torch and gold."

With that, he began to climb with the awkward one-handed grip he had used to descend, but instead of a torch, he held the only hope there was for survival, jewels and gold. As Thomas neared the top, he tried to block fear from his mind. *There would be so little time and but a single chance to save themselves. One misstep and Katherine would die . . .*

He stepped onto firm ground.

"Yes?" Rashim demanded.

Thomas threw the gold and jewels on the floor of the cave.

Sparkles of light flashed.

The bandits—whose lives were built on greed—would have been inhuman if they could have resisted the impulse to look downward at the glittering of wealth.

In that heartbeat, Thomas threw open his cloak, tossed a sword—handle first—at Sir William, and without pausing, charged his left shoulder into Rashim's stomach. As his legs drove forward, Thomas was reaching into his cloak with his right hand for the second sword.

Rashim fell backward. His knife clattered against the ground.

"Run, Katherine!" Thomas shouted, then whirled, sword in front, to help Sir William.

And at that moment, the world seemed to come to an end.

A great light exploded in Thomas' eyes.

He staggered and reeled as a wave of heat roared past him. If he screamed, he could not hear it among the screams of panic from the bandits.

Then, as the echoes of thunder died, and as his eyes began to adjust to the new darkness, he saw them in the light of the fallen torches. Phantoms. Twice the size of a man. Floating downward toward him.

The bandits fell face down on the ground in terror.

Thomas, dazed, barely realized he still carried his sword.

Sir William, whose back was to the phantoms, reacted quickly to the sudden surrender of the bandits. He kicked their swords into the pit and stood above them, ready to strike any who might awkwardly try to rise.

And still the phantoms descended in the dying light.

Rashim began to babble in terror, drool smearing the side of his face.

"Will . . . Will . . . William," Thomas finally managed to say.

Although he had remained standing, the explosion and the appearance of the ghostly spectres and taken away his voice.

Sir William turned his head, just as the first phantom drifted into him. He laughed, and swung his sword into it.

Thomas blinked.

The weapon had slashed through white cloth.

A voice reached them from the darkness.

"Forgive me," the voice said, "I could think of no other way to prepare for your arrival."

Thomas thought of the footprint, the line of dark powder along the edge of the pit. *That bitter taste! Charcoal, sulfur, and potassium nitrate. Explosive powder.*

He found himself grinning. Only a Merlin would have

knowledge of this secret from the far east land of Cathay.

And the phantoms. Cloth supported by a framework of branches. Thomas himself had once been fooled by the same trick. At a campfire. In England. By an old man who had traveled with Katherine.

A protest of disbelief arose then quit unspoken in his throat. *The old man is dead,* Thomas wanted to utter, *the old man died the next morning along the campfire.*

But a figure emerged from the darkness. A familiar stooped and hooded figure which had haunted so many of Thomas' dreams. The old man who had once seemed to know Thomas' every step.

Could Thomas believe what he saw? That the old man was not dead?

The answer came from Katherine.

She ran past the prone bandits and threw her arms around the old man.

"My child," the old man soothed. "If only I could have sent word."

"You are here," Katherine said over and over again. "You are here and alive."

When their embrace finally ended, the old man stepped past Katherine to face Sir William and Thomas.

"It appears you had little need of assistance," the old man said. "I could have waited in St. Jean d'Acre for your return. The leisure would have served my bones much better than travel alone and unobserved through this harsh land."

Sir William grinned. "Hardly. We had not yet won this sword fight. And an entire army pursues us."

The old man dismissed that danger with a wave of hand. "Bah. An army in pursuit of us will be like a horse chasing a gnat."

He then pointed at Thomas. "Sir William, the young man

has proven himself as I predicted."

Thomas bowed his head in respect. Inwardly, he was not as calm. Thoughts raced through his mind. *Memories. Possibilities. The old man had known their destination—this cave. The old man had been in the Holy Land the entire time. He knew with sudden certainty that the old man was . . .*

Thomas barely dared raise his head to ask.

When he did, Thomas found himself staring into the eyes of the old man, for the hood had been thrown back. Thomas found himself staring at a man now not stooped, now standing with the solid strength of a man barely older than Sir William. Thomas found himself staring through the flickering light at a gentle smile in a face that was eerily familiar.

Thomas did not have a chance to ask his question.

For the man answered it as his smile widened with joy.

"Hello, my son," he said to Thomas. "It has been a long wait."

KATHERINE
Dungeon of Despair

MIDSUMMER A. D. 1314

Katherine reached above her shoulders with one hand and—only for a moment—gathered and squeezed her hair into a thick ponytail between her fingers. She released the hair almost immediately, and took satisfaction to feel its weight fall upon her shoulders. *Barely a year ago,* she thought, *I had borrowed shears to cut this ragged and short. Never again . . . one cannot pose as a lady while looking like a boy.*

Then, almost unconsciously, she smoothed her dress with quick pats and tugs.

"Have no fear, m'lady," Thomas said. "You are a sight to ravage the hearts of men and to send jealousy quivering through the ladies of the court."

"Thomas," she scolded, for he had guessed correctly at her nervousness. "Must you peer at my innermost thoughts?"

"All these months of travel together . . . " he shrugged. "Not once have I seen you so concerned about your appearance."

Katherine softened. *Indeed, all these months of travel together.*

Moments of extreme danger as they had avoided Mameluke soldiers in the Holy Land, fought wayside bandits, survived the most vicious storms at sea. Hours of conversation during the quieter times—beside evening campfires or on a ship's deck shifting to the waves beneath starlight. How could they not know each other? Yet they had avoided talk of the one thing nearest their hearts—love for the other—because, she could only guess, they each feared what might come to pass in England should the Druids be victors. And now, they were about to take the first step into the final battle—which if won might finally free them to dream of something more together than the companionship of fellow soldiers. Now, they were about to take the first step into the final battle, and all she had as a weapon was her appearance.

"Thomas," she said, "Look about you. Is this not reason enough to have concern about the manner in which others will perceive us?"

To please her, Thomas made an exaggerated pretense of scanning the Tower, the walls, and courtyard. She knew full well it had already been done; his eyes always took in every detail as he walked.

Behind them lay the rest of London, with its narrow twisted streets of cobblestone, hundreds of merchant's shops, beggars, pickpockets, musicians, storytellers, scoundrels, homeless urchins, and countless thousands of others who made the city vibrate with life and noise and stink and joy and sorrow.

Ahead, across the moat that separated the royal residence from the city, sat a half dozen buildings of smoothed stone blocks. The huge gate was open, so that the interior was visible from where they stood. Some buildings were connected by hallways, some centered alone and away from the high circling walls, and all easily larger than most castles found on countryside estates. The forbidding wall, circled by a moat all around, emcompassed an area the size of a small village, which in fact, this was.

The royal residences. A part of London, yet separate because of the nobility who lived within, these majestic buildings sat on the north bank of the Thames River. Barely a month before, Katherine, the knight, Thomas, and his father had finally arrived at the nearby London docks on the same river. As their ship had slowly moved upstream against the Thames, they all stood on the deck, drinking in the sounds and sights of London. From that vantage point, they had seen the top half of the most imposing building within the walls, the Tower. Even then, within the safety of the ship, Katherine shivered at the sight.

The Tower.

This building, high and mighty with cramped windows cut into the stone, held the political prisoners of the King of England—Edward the Second—who himself lived in luxury less than a hundred yards away in his permanent residence. It was said King Edward often enjoyed a stroll past it after a meal, that it helped his digestion to hear the cries of agony and pleas for mercy from his enemies within.

Yet it was not simply this awesome display of wealth and power that caused Katherine to wonder how she might appear to others.

All of the people within sight were dressed in colorful silk finery. The women, with their long flowing gowns and tight bodices, were assisted by maids who ensured their skirts did not drag on the ground. Some of the bolder ladies even wore tall, pointed hats to follow the latest fashion.

The men also had taken great pains to avoid the warm, practical dress of poor peasants. Almost as if to prove their distance from such lesser creatures—who wore comfortable loose breeches as Thomas did now—the nobles wore tights.

Their tunics were short and brightly colored.

The men and women strolled through the grounds accompanied by their forced laughter and highly expensive greyhounds.

It was a spectacle which gave little comfort to Katherine. She shuddered at the prospect of dealing with the intrigue of the high court. But it had to be done, for it might take them days to accomplish what they so desperately needed.

They wanted an audience with King Edward himself.

13

"Must this servant accompany you *every* day?" sniffed the slim courtier as he pointed at Thomas. "Your beauty and dress show royal blood, of course, but your choice of menservants. . . ."

The courtier let his voice trail away with a sniff, then continued, "Each morning for the last ten mornings I've had to suffer this peasant's . . ." the courtier searched for words capable of conveying restrained outrage " . . . this peasant's unspeakable coarseness in dress and attitude. *What* on earth will Duke Whittingham think of me when I present such a peasant along with a lady like you? After all, a chamberlain does not receive just anybody, and Duke Whittingham is no exception."

Katherine noticed that Thomas tried to maintain the sullen look of a dull peasant. She knew him well enough to catch the twinkle in his eye, and she knew him well enough to understand what he thought of the courtier's yellow tights and effeminate manners and voice.

She was glad, however, that Thomas maintained the long suffering expression of a servant accustomed to abuse, and she smiled sweetly at the courtier. "This servant is my best defense as I travel through dangerous streets."

"Really?" The courtier arched a critical eyebrow.

"Yes," Katherine replied. "Already, he has killed three men with his bare hands."

The courtier jumped back slightly in alarm. Thomas growled. The courtier scurried farther away.

Thomas growled again and Katherine bit back a giggle.

The courtier nearly fell over himself as he tried to back all the way down the corridor, too terrified to turn his eyes away from Thomas. The courtier reached a corner and disappeared. A moment later, only his head appeared, and he gasped out one last sentence.

"The chamberlain will see you when the bells strike the next hour!" With that, the courtier pulled his head from sight. The pattering of his feet quickly retreating down the hallway was audible enough to draw a smile from Thomas.

"That is not a man," Thomas said, "it is a mouse. What kind of king have we who surrounds himself with the like?"

"Shush," Katherine said. "Sir William warned us the royal court would have its share of groveling flatterers and shameless bribe-takers."

"This one is both," Thomas spat. "For all the gold you have given him, I cannot believe it has taken ten days just to see the king's administrator. What price to finally reach the king himself?"

"It matters little," Katherine said as she sat straighter on the wooden bench. "Not many receive an audience with the chamberlain, let alone King Edward. We cannot—"

She stopped abruptly as two ladies and a nobleman approached. The nobleman bowed at Katherine while the two ladies pointedly ignored her behind their waving fans.

"Word of your beauty has reached many," Thomas observed out of the side of his mouth as they passed. "The ladies here are less than friendly."

Katherine felt herself redden in the beginnings of a blush at his devilish grin. But she could not deny his observation. More than once during their hours of waiting in this remote castle hallway had noblemen stopped with flimsy excuses for their sudden presence, only to be dragged away minutes later by attending ladies.

Moments later they were alone again, and Katherine resumed her spoken thoughts.

"Thomas, we will only have one chance to present the reasons for an audience with the king. We cannot fail now."

"Have you not the book?"

"Of course. You bear the burden of its weight every day as we take it here."

"Then fear none," Thomas said. "It is proof enough for the king to take action against the Druids. And no longer will we fight alone."

"Yet—"

"Yet it is enough. You will tell the chamberlain how we found the book and what it contains. The Druids will no longer move in secrecy. And without that secrecy—their greatest weapon—we will prove victorious."

Katherine knew Thomas spoke true. *She had rehearsed again and again their urgent story for King Edward. No mention would be made of Merlins, only of the Druids. She would tell him that—*

The church bells rang, a sound that echoed clearly in the silence of the hallway. Almost instantly, the courtier appeared at the corner. He moved no closer, only beckoned from that safe position.

Katherine followed, with Thomas close behind.

Let my words impress, she prayed silently. *Let them strike truer than any arrows.*

The courtier led them through a maze of corridors, then stopped at an arched doorway. Two guards stood in the recess of the doorway; each solemnly stepped aside at the impatient snapping of the courtier's fingers.

"Go inside," the courtier said as he pushed open the large double doors. "And expect no more than ten minutes of audience."

Katherine swept past him, snorting with quiet amusement to see how the courtier kept ample distance between himself and Thomas.

The doors shut behind them.

It was a luxurious enough chamber to contain its own fireplace, now filled with dead white ashes of a fire long past. A portrait of King Edward the Second hung on the wall above the fireplace. Tapestries of deer hunts lined the other walls, and, on the far side of the room, an upright divider—much like the dividers used in dressing chambers—hid the rear portion of the chamber. One large chair, with leather armrests and footstool, dominated the center of the room.

No one awaited them.

"Strange," Thomas said to Katherine. "I assumed the Duke Whittingham would be here. It seems all these royal riffraff rush to and fro at such a frightful pace, that he would be anxious to hear us and send us off again."

"Not when he hears my words," Katherine vowed. "It—"

She was interrupted by the opening of the doors.

A large, stoop-shouldered man in a purple cloak entered the chamber. He bowed once, then stood near the chair, and placed one foot upon the footstool.

"You have begged audience," he said. And waited.

"For good reason," Katherine said. She drew a deep

breath. "My servant carries a book which has lain undisturbed in the Holy Land since the time of Roman soldiers. This book contains proof of a secret circle of false sorcerers and their plot which now threatens England and the good King Edward."

The large man leaned forward, so that his elbow rested on the knee elevated by his stance upon the footstool.

"My dear child," the large man said. "If you meant to intrigue me with such a bold opening statement, you have succeeded. Not that—with a countenance as lovely as yours—you need such a strategy to hold a man's attention."

Katherine half bowed in a courtsey to accept the compliment, and hoped Thomas would do no more than clench his fists as he did now.

"My lord," she said quickly, "my words are truth."

"Indeed," the man said with a voice of honey. "Continue."

Katherine began her explanation much as Thomas had done in convincing Rashim that a treasure did exist. She told of the time before the Romans conquered, when Druids ruled the land. She told of the Druid secrets of science and astronomy, and their secrecy, and of the Roman general who plundered their great wealth, only to be summoned to the Holy Land, where the wealth lay hidden in the Cave of Letters for so many centuries. She explained how bandits had taken them, and how Mameluke soldiers had followed along the shore of the Dead Sea.

The large man held up a hand glittering with large rings. Katherine stopped.

"How did you come into possession of this remarkable knowledge?" he asked. "And how is it you have just now returned with your story? We lost the Holy Lands to the infidels a generation ago."

"My father was a Crusader knight," Katherine said. "Forsaken in the Holy Land when the infidels defeated our armies. I was raised there, hidden among the peoples."

She gestured to take in her fine apparel and the jewelry around her neck.

"I do not have royal blood, as your courtier might have assumed. Rather, the treasure that my father found provided me with passage here and with the clothes I needed to gain entrance into royal society."

The large man closed his eyes in thought. Without opening them he said, "You and he found this treasure in a cave. You were—as you had been saying—you were held hostage by bandits and pursued by Mameluke soldiers. How did you escape with treasure?"

"The bandits were overcome with greed," she said. "My father and this servant were able to overcome them. We left the bandits in the pit in the cave for the soldiers to find."

The large man opened his eyes in sudden surprise. "For the soldiers to find?"

"Yes." Katherine explained how the soldiers had been tricked into following the main party of bandits. "As we left the cave and trekked through the ravine back to the Dead Sea, we dropped pieces of gold and jewelry, so that there was a trail of treasure to lead back to the cave. When we reached the shore of the Dead Sea, we turned north. The soldiers, instead of pursuing us along the shore line, followed the treasure back to the cave, where they would be rewarded by the bulk of the treasure, and by the sight of bandits held helpless beside that treasure at the bottom of the pit."

"Splendid!" the large man clapped his hands. "Absolutely splendid!"

His craggy face then became a frown of puzzlement. "Did you not feel dismay to leave such wealth behind?"

"Not when it meant our lives to attempt to keep it all," Katherine said. "Besides, what we could carry ourselves was enough. And. . . ."

Katherine paused. This was the most important moment.

" . . . and there was the book. The Druid book. It contains—"

"Nothing but the fanciful spinning of a fairytale!" came a booming voice from behind the divider.

The large man dropped his foot from the footstool and straightened to ramrod stiff attention.

"Duke Whittingham," the large man whispered. "I did not know . . ."

"Think nothing of it," the Duke said as he stepped from behind the divider. "You had your instructions. Pretend to listen to these impostors. You could not know that I too wanted to listen in secrecy. But I have heard enough."

Katherine barely registered those words, for the shock of recognition of the speaker hit her like the blow of a sword.

Waleran.

"Waleran!" The uttering of his name was a low hiss, but it did not come from her lips.

Instead, it was like a curse from Thomas, as he too, reeled with shock.

"You are dismissed," Duke Whittingham said to the large man.

"Yes, m'lord." He bowed quickly, then almost ran from the chamber. The doors slammed shut behind him.

Waleran. An ugly man with a half-balding forehead above cheeks rounded like those of a well-stuffed chipmunk. Ears lumpy and thick, so large they almost flapped. And hair which fell scraggly and greasy onto sloped shoulders. Not even now, dressed in royal robes, did he have a single redeeming feature to lighten his appearance of fetid evil.

"You would do well not to call me Waleran," he said. "Duke Whittingham is my title. And let me assure you, I have ways to punish those who do not address me properly."

Katherine opened her mouth once, then shut it. Her thoughts were in such disarray, she was unable to find words.

"That is better," Waleran said with a cruel leer, misinterpreting her silence as obedience. "You might have been able to escape me in the Holy Land, but you shall not be so fortunate twice."

14

"You are such fools," Waleran laughed. His teeth were unevenly spaced, and black with rot. "So easy to deceive."

"How . . . how can the king's chamberlain . . ." Katherine stopped, still nearly faint from surprise.

"How can the king's chamberlain be a Druid? Or how can the king's chamberlain accomplish so much as a Druid?"

Katherine nodded. *Waleran here was not what they had expected during the long months of voyage and planning.*

"Should it not be obvious? It is I who oversee all the Druid actions. And who better placed to oversee a kingdom than the right-hand man of the king himself? And why should you show such surprise? You know the Druids have penetrated all levels of society. Surely it would seem logical that a Druid attain the position of chamberlain. Especially when the previous chamberlain was a Druid. As was the previous. The unquestioned authority of this position gives great freedom and—" Waleran snapped his mouth shut and dropped his hand to his sword.

"Young man," he said to Thomas with a voice promising death, "sit. Yes, immediately. On the cold floor. From there, you shall have difficulty continuing your attempted slow movement toward me."

Thomas hesitated.

"Do you think it was an accident that you were searched? I know you do not have a weapon and mine—" Waleran unsheathed his sword "—is coated with poison." He paused. "Now sit! Or watch Katherine die."

Thomas lowered himself onto the stone floor with great reluctance.

"Much better." Waleran cackled, then broke into a wheeze. When he recovered his breath, he moved to the large chair in the center of the room, and placed his sword beside him on the armrest. "I shall satisfy your curiosity. In turn, you shall satisfy mine."

More like you shall gloat, Katherine thought.

"As you well know," Waleran said. "It was I who posed as a fellow prisoner in the dungeon of Magnus during the time that Thomas and Sir William spent in captivity."

Waleran scowled. "I overheard nothing about that which we seek."

Katherine grinned inside. *Thomas kept his vow well. What still lay hidden in the monastery of his childhood might . . .*

"I overheard nothing about that which we seek," Waleran repeated, "and a freak whose face was burned helped them escape."

Again, Katherine found reason for hidden satisfaction. *He does not know it was I behind those bandages.*

"It was hardly worth my efforts for what little I gained in that prison." Waleran squirmed as if remembering the dank darkness, flea-infested, straw and the scurrying of rats. "However, my time in York paid dividends, as you know."

Katherine bowed her head. *Waleran had been in a neighboring cell as she spoke to the captured Duke of York. What he had heard was enough to. . . .*

Waleran cackled again. "Yes. Thomas here thought he was so brave and noble, capturing Isabelle and holding her as hostage. Little did he know we had deliberately allowed that, so that he would lead us to—"

You saw the old man dead," Thomas interrupted with bitterness. "Was that not enough?"

Katherine kept her head bowed, this time, however, so that Waleran would not see the gleam of triumph in her eyes. Yes, Thomas had led Waleran's soldiers to her and the old man. But the old man, in the confusion of the attack, had pretended death by swallowing one of the prepared pills he always carried among the herbs and potions beneath his cloak. This one was made from the dried and crushed bark of rhododendrons, which caused unconsciousness, coldness of skin, and a vastly reduced heart rate. Yes it had been a gamble, for any of the soldiers might have run him through with a sword, but a necessary gamble. Once the Druids were convinced the old man was dead. . . .

"Dead, and not a moment too soon," Waleran laughed. "His death made it easy to out maneuver you two. Following you both to the Holy Land was child's play. And such simple minds." Waleran choked on his laughter, then recovered. "Should it not be obvious that if the Merlins had men in the Holy Land, the Druids would also have their spies."

"Lord Hubert Baldwin," Thomas spat.

"None other," Waleran said, bowing at the waist from his position in the chair. "One of your most trusted men and one of our greater allies. Without his help, Magnus might never have fallen as it first did."

Katherine felt frozen to the ground. *So many died then. A*

generation of Merlins wiped out. And now the Druids would be able to move openly against an entire country.

She lifted her head.

"You gave Lord Baldwin his instructions in Jericho."

"Of course, m'lady," came the mocking reply. "He is a man of strong arm, but limited intelligence. And I did not want to soil my own hands with such matters."

"You mean you did not want to risk your life," Thomas said. "Baldwin now rots in a Jerusalem dungeon."

"So I've been told." Waleran shrugged. "No matter. I needed to return immediately to England—as a chamberlain I have freedom but not *unlimited* freedom—and the situation seemed to be in hand. He was a fool to allow himself to be taken in Jersualem."

Then Waleran grinned, an ugly evil grin of stinking breath and smug triumph. "You have reported the rest. What he failed to do, you accomplished for us. What we lost so many centuries ago, you recovered and against all odds, returned to England."

He stood and rubbed his hands briskly. "I shall take the book now," he said.

With reluctance, Katherine nodded at Thomas.

"Not so, my dear," Waleran said. "*You* take the book from him and slowly hand it to me. He is young enough and strong enough to attempt an attack."

Waleran placed his hand on the swords hilt as he directed his words at Katherine. "And if *you* attempt anything, I shall run you through."

Thomas removed the book from its wrappings. Katherine took it with both hands and extended it to Waleran.

He merely smiled.

"You think I will reach for it and drop my guard? Not so. Place it on the armrest and step away."

Katherine did as instructed.

When she had retreated to her previous position, Waleran opened the book and glanced inside.

"Ahh. Splendid," he breathed. "I see already many of the secrets we lost over the centuries."

He ran a dirty finger down one of the pages. "Here. A mixture of common garden herbs to induce madness... there, a prediction of the stars movement, knowledge to impress superstitious peasants."

Waleran paused. "But you already know these weapons. The eclipse during the hanging of the knight. That was masterful." He mused farther. "Of course, the old man is dead and I need not worry...."

He slammed his fist down on the book, and Katherine's head snapped upward in attention.

"Tell me," his voice was now ugly and threatening, "what did you hope to accomplish with this book?"

Katherine bit her tongue.

"Tell me!" Waleran roared. "Silence gains you nothing!"

He leapt to his feet and placed the tip of his sword against Katherine's throat.

"I need only pierce the skin," Waleran said, in a voice unexpectedly silky, "and she dies. So tell me."

"At the back," Thomas said hurriedly. "At the back of the book lies the Druid outline for means of taking a country. Key towns to hold. Key people to bribe. Although it is dated by the passage of centuries, it shows intent. Proof of a Druid masterplan, to be delivered to King Edward. That, and news of what is happening in northern towns now, was to be enough for him to consider a Druid threat in this day and age. With his help, we hoped to stop you."

"Children, children," Waleran said with insincere sympathy as he stepped away from Katherine and sat once again in his chair. "What delusions you carry. King Edward himself is a pliable fool, who relies heavily on my advice. And he is so distracted now with war against Scotland, that I am allowed to dictate our domestic affairs."

Waleran laughed. "Do you think it is an accident that Scotland preoccupies him? Hardly. Once again, my advice. As I said, a useful distraction." Waleran then sighed and stared into the distance. When he spoke again, it was with the voice of a parent lecturing a child.

"Thomas," he said, "you have my thanks for securing this valuable book. But we need more from you. First, the Cup of the Holy Grail. You took it when you kidnapped Isabelle. We did not find it in your possession when we recaptured you and killed the old man."

The silence was heavy.

"More than that too," Waleran said softly. "Give what we have always wanted from you. What you were entrusted to guard since birth."

Still Thomas sat silent.

"You have a simple choice," Waleran said. "Join us and gain the wealth and power of the land's most powerful earl. Or remain silent and see Katherine die."

"No!" Katherine uttered. "My life is nothing compared to what he seeks. Thomas, I die gladly."

"Thomas?" Waleran purred.

Still Thomas said nothing.

"A difficult choice?" Waleran asked. "Perhaps time in the torture chambers will loosen your tongue."

Waleran did not wait for a response.

Instead, he raised his voice. "Guards!"

The door opened instantly.

Waleran stood and pointed to Thomas and Katherine. "Take them to the Tower."

15

Katherine wept freely. Though she was not alone in the Tower prison cell, her cries went unheard. The other occupant of the cell was Thomas, unconscious. Moments before, two guards had dragged him in, his head sagged like a broken puppet. They had shackled him—one chain bracketed to each wrist—in his place along the wall.

Now, the chains kept him from falling forward completely. His hands, attached to the chains, were behind his back, and Katherine hardly dared guess how much it tore his muscles to have his entire weight straining so awkwardly against his chest and arms.

She reached for his face.

She didn't need the clank of chains which followed her every movement to remind her that it was near impossible. From where she stood, she could only move a foot away from the wall. Her own wrists were shackled as well; with lifted arm reaching and pushing against the chain, her fingers stopped inches short of Thomas' face.

"My love," she cried, "awake."

He did not.

Tears streamed down her cheeks. Five days running the guards had taken him away during midmorning. Five days running, they had returned him less than an hour later. Each time he had been placed unconscious in those chains. Each time it had taken him longer to return to consciousness.

She longed to touch his face. In sudden rage, Katherine yanked her chains, uncaring of the stabbing pain of the cruel metal of the shackles biting into the softness of her wrist. But her fingers fell tantalizing inches short.

"Thomas," she whispered again. "Please. Please wake."

In the quiet, a rat rustled in the straw at her feet. She cared little. Rats were as common as the fleas, and her attention was on Thomas' pale face, motionless in the sunlight that fell through a high, narrow window.

Thomas stirred. Groaned. Blinked. And slowly found his feet.

"Katherine," he croaked. Joy filled his voice. "You are still there."

She turned her head so that he would not see the tears. *How could he think of her first when they inflicted so much pain upon him?*

"I am still here," she said, her voice muffled by the hair which clung to her wet cheeks.

"Thank our Lord," he said. "It is my worst nightmare. That I will return to here and find you gone. I . . . I . . . could not bear this prison alone."

"Neither I," she said simply.

She brought her face around again to the sound of the shuffling of his chains.

They stared at each other.

Thomas brought his hand up, as she did hers. Wordless

they reached for the other, but the chains brought them short. Their fingertips could get no closer than six inches apart.

"I dreamed you called me 'my love,' " Thomas said.

"I did," Katherine replied. She waited long moments, as if debating whether to speak. "It is a subject we have avoided," she said. "My love for you. Yours, I pray for me. My own fear was this. To declare love for you yet be helpless against the Druids."

"We are not helpless," Thomas vowed. "For I have not revealed to the torturers the secrets of my childhood monastery."

He scowled. "Not even the location of that monastery."

"To save your life. . . ."

"No. Sir William hinted that my knowledge could turn the final battle. To reveal it now means my life is worthless."

"Yet—"

"No, Katherine. There is no 'yet.' " He grinned. It was flash of white from a pain-exhausted face. Blood trickled from one corner of his mouth. "We shall watch for escape."

Thomas raised his voice as anger overtook. "I have said it before. We shall watch for escape. Then, we shall return to the monastery, and I will solve the final puzzle, find what it is the Druids so badly seek! With that, they shall be defeated."

The effort of rage cost him his reserves of energy. Briefly, he sagged again against the chains. "Then we shall talk of our love," he finished softly. "Then we shall talk of our love."

Katherine wept again, this time unable to hide her tears.

Thomas gritted his teeth and clenched his fists. Anger once more gave him strength to stand upright.

"Katherine," he began. "Do not despair. You will see a chance for escape. Or I will." His voice rose again. "All we need do is reach the monastery. That will–"

Thomas stopped as a key turned in the lock.

A huge, fat surly guard–the one who shoved food at them daily–kicked open the door. From behind him, sounded a blare of royal trumpets.

"Make way for the King!" came a shout. A courtier dashed inside the prison cell.

Then, without further fanfare, King Edward the Second, the reigning monarch of all England, stepped through the doorway.

He was a tall, powerfully built man with fair skin and reddish blond hair. He carried the royal scepter, so brilliantly studded with jewels of all colors that his purple robes and white-furred collar seemed poor in comparison.

He stood still and stared at them, his face completely empty of all emotion.

Katherine felt a shiver go through her. *This man need only lift a finger, and we are free. Or dead. At his command, armies of thousands march upon towns and villages.*

"This is the traitor with the tongue of stone," King Edward observed.

"Your majesty, I–" Thomas began to say.

The courtier stepped forward and slapped Thomas across the face.

"One does not address his majesty unless asked a direct question."

"I am not–"

Another slap. This one rocked Thomas back against the wall.

Katherine's eyes filled with tears again.

"I am not a traitor!" Thomas roared.

The courtier prepared to strike Thomas again.

"Enough," King Edward said.

The courtier stepped away. King Edward moved forward to examine Thomas.

"I am told our best men cannot break your spirit."

Thomas raised his head tall and met the King's eyes. "Innocence gives strength, m'lord."

"Indeed," King Edward said noncommittally. He turned to examine Katherine.

"And you," he said to her, "are as beautiful as the rumors hint."

Then he walked away from them both, and filled the doorway again.

"I have heard many declarations of innocence," King Edward said. "From men as brave as you. From men who have endured the very chains you wear. Indeed, often I think it takes greater bravery to be a traitor, than serve the king. For traitors know the terrible price they will pay."

Katherine's eyes were on Thomas. He opened his mouth to speak.

"No." With the full weight of royal authority, King Edward's command halted any words.

"There is nothing you can say to convince me," King Edward continued. "The Duke of Whittingham has told me enough, and if I cannot trust him . . ." King Edward shrugged as he made his jest. "If I cannot trust him, my kingdom is worthless."

Such irony. Katherine wanted to shriek. But she, like Thomas, knew it would sound like the ravings of lunatics, any talk of Druids and Merlins and kingdom-wide conspiracies. Without the book, they had no hope of presenting their case. In chains, against the word of the King's chamberlain, they had even less hope.

King Edward fixed Thomas with a hard stare. Then Katherine.

"Why am I here, you might well ask, for I refuse to hear your case." King Edward paused. "Not for curiosity, be assured."

His voice became quiet with menace.

"My son has been kidnapped," he said. "I have many enemies, all linked to the prisoners here, and I am here to tell each prisoner the same, so that word may spread and my son be returned. My royal proclamation is this. King Edward the Third is returned safe within a week, or all prisoners within the Tower shall be beheaded."

16

They were fed twice each day. In the morning, their guard brought a bowl of thin, fly-specked porridge. In the early evening, it was bread—quite often drilled with holes burrowed by beetles—and a bowl of beans boiled to mush.

The guard was so large that he had to squeeze sideways to get into the cell. That action usually forced him to spill a major portion from the bowls he juggled. Worse, their guard enjoyed too much beer throughout the afternoon, and this led to more unsteadiness.

There was nothing unexpected about his arrival for the evening meal. He would jangle his keys for several minutes and fumble with the lock, then kick the door open, and grunt his way into the cell.

That he always drank too much beer was evident by the foul breath which somehow overwhelmed the usual stench of the cramped prison cell. His eyes were bleary and his nose a brilliant red. Because he was so large in the small cell, most of his movements meant collision with Katherine or Thomas.

Three nights closer to the eve of their execution, Katherine and Thomas received their usual warning of his arrival.

The door clanged open and the guard struggled through. This time, however, he strained harder than normal to wheeze air into his lungs. His eyes were unfocused and his entire face the red usually restricted only to his nose.

He bent to place one bowl at Thomas' feet, and barely managed to keep his balance. He then turned to Katherine. He smiled uncertainly and his breath made her choke. His large stubbled face loomed closer, his double chins wobbled.

I'm glad my stomach is so pinched that any food will do, she thought, *for this sight would dull the keenest hunger.*

Her thoughts turned to sudden alarm. For the ugly face did not stop its approach.

This is not an attempted kiss! It was not.

The big man sagged forward and fell into Katherine. His bear-like arms engulfed her.

"Thomas!" she tried to shout, but the guard's weight suffocated any words which might have left her lungs.

The stench of his unwashed clothing gagged her, the rubbery feel of his flesh nauseated her, and still he pressed against her into the wall.

She tried to beat her arms against his chest, but she was pinned too securely. Yet his weight was passive, as if he were not attacking, but had . . . *collapsed?*

As if answering her thoughts, he rolled downward and fell in a heap at her feet. Katherine found herself staring at the ring of keys on the guard's belt.

She hardly believed this might be. Slowly, she reached down and tugged on the keys.

The guard did not respond.

It took Katherine less than a minute to find the key which unshackled her wrists.

17

"Home!" Thomas shouted. "I . . . am . . . home!"

His long drawn out words echoed throughout the valley below from where Katherine and he stood at a vantage point among the shadows of large rocks.

The valley itself was narrow and compressed—with more rock and stunted trees on the slopes than sweet grass and sheep—a direct contrast to the richer and wider valleys to the south. Like most of the land around, it belonged to a large order of Cistercian monks. Yet unlike the land farther south, time had proven the valley too poor, and barely worth the investment of an obscure abbey hall, library, and living quarters made from stone quarried directly from the nearby hills.

From their vantage point, towering trees blurred the walls of the abbey hall. It was, as Katherine knew, the monastery where Thomas had been raised, believing the entire time he was an orphan.

"Home!" he shouted again. Birds scattered from a nearby bush.

"Thomas!" She tried to sound angry but could not. His joy was too contagious. After all, they had survived a hurried trek through most of England to reach these moors so close to Magnus.

"There is none to hear me," Thomas said. "The monks have long since left." He grinned. "You'll remember the cause of that."

She did. It had been the start of his path of conquering Magnus, the beginning of all that had led to this moment above the valley.

"Come on," he whispered, as if conspiring. "Let me show you the way."

Thomas moved quickly from the exposed summit into the trees. Katherine knew from their conversations during the 10 days it had taken to travel this far north of London that years of avoiding the harsh monks had taught Thomas every secret deer path in these surrounding hills.

She was barely able to keep pace. At times, Thomas would approach a seemingly solid stand of brush, then slip sideways into an invisible opening among the jagged branches and later reappear quietly farther down the hill.

"Hurry," he called.

The man is almost skipping like a boy.

Katherine smiled at his enthusiasm. No matter their troubles, here was a time to set them aside, and for a moment enjoy the sunshine, the feel of grass against ankle, the song of the babble of the tiny river which ran past the abbey.

Their first destination was not the abbey itself.

Instead, Thomas moved directly to the river, and stood at its bank. The moss of the rocks beneath the water waved in the current like tails of tiny fish.

"You know about the cave, do you not?" Thomas asked her.

Katherine nodded. "The old man—your father—and I once waited for you here. It was an agony, to not be sure whether you were Druid or Merlin, to not be able to simply join you instead of follow."

"We are together now." But he said it in such a dismissing way that Katherine knew Thomas did not want to discuss the reason for that mistrust, so she too lost herself in thought.

If his mother had not died while training him here to be a Merlin, she would have been able to impart so many more secrets as he came of age. Instead, with her unexpected death, Thomas had struggled so long in the belief that he was alone, and unaware of his destiny as a Merlin. And we, in our isolation, feared that the Druids had found him in this obscure abbey, and had managed to turn him against us.

When Katherine looked at Thomas again, she saw his eyes were closed, his head bowed.

Minutes later, he lifted his head. "She was a remarkable woman," Thomas finally said. "There is much that I owe her."

Then, to dispel the somber mood, he smiled. "Never would I have dreamed that I would regard this abbey with fondness."

He pointed past the abbey. "The pond there? Many was the time I could not be found by those wretched monks. Little did they know I was beneath the water, that I excelled at breathing through a reed."

He pointed at the massive gray walls of the abbey itself. "My bed chamber was there, that tiny window. I slept on a straw mattress placed atop a great wooden trunk. At nights, I escaped down those walls."

He laughed at the surprise on her face. "No, I was not a fly. There are enough cracks between the stones for a determined—and much smaller—boy to find room for fingers and toes."

She laughed with him. And marveled at how his gray eyes seemed almost blue beneath the clear skies.

What a dream. That he and I could one day be together and never be on guard. If only our last desperate actions will—

"We have stood here long enough?" Thomas asked.

She nodded.

Thomas turned, and led her to the cave.

Several bends upstream from the abbey hall, comfortably shaded by large oaks, there stood beside the water a jumble of rocks and boulders, some as large as a peasant's hut. Among them, a freak of nature had created a dry cool cave, its narrow entrance concealed by jutting slabs of granite and bushes rising from softer ground below.

The knight will be waiting for us, Katherine assured herself as they walked among the boulders. *Surely not everything we planned has gone astray.*

"Count to one thousand," Thomas suddenly said. They were still at the side of the river. Immediately to their left was the entrance, so well concealed it was difficult to see it, even from 10 feet away.

"Count to one thousand? Here? Now?"

Thomas laughed at the confusion that must have passed across her face.

"No. Those were the rules I was taught very young by Sarah. 'Count to one thousand. Watch carefully. Count to one thousand. Then slowly, cautiously, enter. Let no person ever discover this place.' "

Katherine nodded.

"It was a game, I thought then. Sarah taught me patience, how to wait here and listen to the sounds of the surrounding forest until I was part of it."

Thomas closed his eyes, and smiled in recollection. "Inside, so cool, so safe. We spent hours in there. She taught me to read, to understand mathematics, to apply logic."

Katherine smiled in her own recollections. *The ways of a Merlin. What joy there had been to be lost in the wonder of learning. He, here in a cave in a tiny valley in the vast moors of northern England. Me, in a sun-baked town a world away on the edge of the Holy Land. Both of us, with a path destined to bring us to this cave. Would all of it end today or—*

"Has a trampling army arrived?" The voice came from a large figure stepping into sight from the cave's entrance.

"Sir William!" The relief in Katherine's voice surprised her. She had been counting so heavily that indeed he would be waiting here.

"A trampling army?" Thomas snorted. "Are you so old and weak that you need an army to rescue you?"

"Hardly," Sir William said as he accepted Thomas' offer of an extended hand. "Rather, by the sound of your progress, I expected all of England to be outside. You make enough noise to wake the dead."

Then the knight rolled his eyes. "Of course, waking the dead is the least of my concerns. But if you wake the babe-in-arms inside, then all wrath will fall upon us, for his majesty is prone to tantrums of temper most unseemly for one of royalty."

"The babe?" Katherine asked. "He is here? Safe? With his nurse?

Sir William nodded.

"Follow me inside," the knight said. "I will introduce you to the heir of all England, Edward the Third."

18

The cave was not a natural cave. Instead, it resulted from the haphazard piling of huge slabs of granite over the large boulders that lined the river. The cave was barely deeper than the interior of a peasant's hut, and lit by a shaft of sunlight that fell between the cracks of two of the largest slabs that formed the cave's roof. In the far corner, an oily torch burned, its smoke carried immediately upward in a draft that escaped between smaller cracks in the ceiling.

Centuries of the growth of moss and lichens had eroded most of the rock, and, combined with the light from the sun and torch, now made the walls seem softer than mere harsh granite.

Katherine did not have to stoop as she stepped through the entrance, and once inside, she discovered there was room to stretch upward should she have wished.

She did not.

She could have moved to the left side of the cave, to an open chest as high as her knees and wide as a cart.

She did not.

Instead, she stared at the other occupants of the cave.

In the corner, on a rough stool, sat a nurse, shawled in the coarse cloth of a peasant. In her arms, wrapped in the finest linen available, was a baby.

Edward the Third. Less than two years old. Eyes closed. A wisp of dark hair matted to his forehead. Tiny fingers clenched.

"Did his majesty travel well?" Thomas was asking.

Katherine didn't hear Sir William's reply. She was struggling with unfamiliar emotions.

She had been brought up a lonely child. The years she spent behind bandages—disguised as a freak—had ensured she did not play with or meet other children. Never had she been allowed to hold a baby or even creep close.

So here, only steps away, she was mesmerized by both the baby and how it affected her. The baby's vulnerability fascinated her. That same vulnerability also made her yearn to hold and protect.

She did not see the boy as a future king. She simply saw the boy as someone who needed love. So, it seemed, did the nurse, who leaned over the baby and soothed him with low murmuring.

Words echoed in Katherine's mind. Words from Sir William, months earlier as he told her why every Earl of York for generations had obeyed Druid commands and also how this same method would be the final piece of the Druid scheme to conquer England from within. Through clenched teeth, Sir William had explained the punishment to those who might disobey.

The Druids have a simple method to cause such a mysterious death. A potion causes deep sleep and allows an evil one to dab honey in a man's ears, then small maggots are dropped within . . . Katherine, imagine this. The masses of people begin to believe the Priests of the Holy Grail. And at the slightest sign of rebellion, the firstborn of every family dies such a death. Mayhaps even before rebellion, the firstborn of the rulers die in such a way. No man would resist. England would be theirs.

No man would resist? As she stared at the baby, Katherine knew that no *woman* could resist. *The evil horror of false sorcerers so ready to destroy the lives of ones so innocent. . . .*

" . . . the travel presented little difficulty." Katherine realized Sir William was replying to Thomas. "But after our arrival here! I've never known something so small could squall so loud."

Thomas began to smirk, but quickly arranged his face to a more sober expression as he noticed the glare on Katherine's face.

"Exiled here in a cold dark cave with a brutish uncaring knight," Katherine said. "I'd squall too."

"Me thinks rather it was the teething which brought forth such squalls," Sir William said, undaunted by Katherine's flash of temper.

Thomas wisely remained silent.

"Men!" Katherine snapped. She turned to the nurse. "May I help? Does he need anything?"

The nurse shook her head without lifting her face to look at Katherine.

"May I . . . may I . . ." Katherine had become shy.

"Hold him?" the nurse asked.

"Yes."

The nurse nodded.

Katherine did not notice the amused glance between

Thomas and Sir William. None of them noticed a visitor step into the cave, his shoes silent on the soft dirt.

Katherine was halfway to the baby when the new voice stopped her.

"Oh my," the voice taunted. "A touching reunion."

Katherine whirled.

Waleran. It was Waleran. As ugly as a nightmare, and leering the evil smile of rotted teeth he had last flashed as guards had taken Katherine and Thomas from his chamber to the Tower.

"Tsk, tsk," Waleran said as Sir William reached for his sword. "This is no place for rudeness. As you can see, I do not carry a weapon."

Sir William ignored the comment and withdrew his sword.

Waleran released an exaggerated sigh. "Dealing with barbarians is so . . . so . . . fruitless."

He pursed his lips and shook his head. "William, William," he chastised. "Do you think I would be fool enough to enter this den of lions like a helpless lamb?"

Waleran replied to his own question, a man who enjoyed the sound of his own voice.

"Hardly, William," Waleran said. "Outside this cave is an army of twenty. All I need do is raise my voice, and all of you will be dead."

19

"Twenty men," Sir William said. "That matters little if I slit your throat now."

Waleran snorted. "And what will become of your friends? Once I am dead, so are they. Thomas . . . Katherine . . . this baby—"

For a moment, the arrogant coolness across Waleran's face slipped. "That is Edward the Third! The entire kingdom is in an uproar. And you have him here!"

Surprise became a sly smile.

"I beg pardon. *We* have him here. Perhaps you've saved me a great deal of trouble."

Before Waleran could say more, Sir William sheathed his sword.

"You will live," Sir William said as the sword hissed back into place, "but it would be more pleasant to share this cave with a half-rotted pig."

Waleran blustered until he managed to contort his face into a sneer. He pointed at Thomas, then at Katherine. "In the very least, a half-rotted pig has more cunning than these two combined."

"Oh?" Sir William asked with the casualness of a man holding back rage only through supreme effort.

"They believed it was an act of God that their guard suffered a seizure in the midst of their cell, that it was a miracle to escape the Tower through the use of the guard's keys."

Waleran laughed until he coughed. "A miracle? Certainly. A miracle the guard didn't die after the potion I placed in his beer. My biggest fear was that he would collapse before he reached their cell."

"You let us escape deliberately so that you could follow us here," Katherine said quietly. "Just as you once let Thomas escape York to see where that led him."

"Yes, my dear," Waleran said in a patronizing voice. "You catch onto these things so *very* quickly. And would it surprise you that every word you said in that cell reached the ears of a listener?"

Katherine blushed.

"Oh, yes," Waleran said. "Every word. Such a shame. The love you two professed for each other will never flower."

He waved that away as insignificant. "Thomas repeatedly made the mistake of telling you that all he needed was to return to the monastery of his childhood. That here would be revealed the final secrets which might overcome us."

"You overheard our conversations and let us escape, just to track us here?" Thomas sounded as if he were in shock.

"Of course," Waleran said. "Nothing less than routine for the genius mind of someone who is the right hand adviser to the King."

The nurse stirred to comfort the baby who had begun to whimper tiny cries at the harshness of Waleran's voice. Her movement was slight, however, she appeared to be too frightened to look up at Waleran.

"This baby. Edward the Third," Waleran said. "Why was he taken?"

"Desperation," Sir William said, after a long exhalation of breath. "There are so few of us Merlins. After centuries of battling Druids at every turn in secrecy, we decided we would finally seek help and bring the battle to light. We needed a way to convince King Edward that the Druid threat was real. Thomas and Katherine were to deliver to King Edward the ancient manuscript which shows the Druid scheme to take all of England. If King Edward did not accept that as proof, we hoped he would believe Druids had kidnapped this baby. It would get him to look closely at how the towns in the northern part of his kingdom have fallen to Druids posing as Priests of the Holy Grail. With King Edward's help, we would stop you before you gained power."

Waleran chuckled. "What a surprise then, that *I* was there as the king's chamberlain. As you well know, King Edward will never hear of that proof. You are the last of the Merlins, and soon, you will be gone."

Katherine shuddered.

"Already, we have dozens of towns here in the north. Having King Edward's son now as hostage only makes our task easier. And within a year, Druids *will* reign supreme."

Sir William sighed. He began to pace the small area of the cave, running his fingers through his hair in distraction. Finally, he moved to a stool near the nurse, bowed his head in defeat, and spoke.

"We have truly failed. King Edward will receive no proof of your existence. You have his son as hostage. And now, you know the location of this abbey."

Waleran rubbed his hands together.

"Yes," he said. "We have finally found the childhood abbey which hid Thomas for all those years. Even if you don't tell us what we need, it will be found."

"I suspect so," Sir William said sadly, head still bowed.

"Do not suspect. Consider it truth," Waleran said. "There are twenty outside now, and more to arrive."

"More?" Katherine asked.

"I have sent messengers to all parts of England. The highest members of our circle will gather here. My original intentions were to gather our best minds to find what you had hidden here. Furthermore, it seems it will give us a chance to direct the final stages of battle. England will be ours. This baby here will be the heir to nothing."

Thomas finally spoke. His voice was tinged with bitterness. "Druid leaders will all meet in secrecy here?"

Waleran laughed. "You *do* see the irony. This obscure abbey was sufficient to hide you for years, even from the all-seeing eyes of the Druid web. How much better then, for us to gather in the same remoteness?"

"All is lost," Sir William said. "The Druids have conquered the Merlins."

Katherine moved to him and placed a comforting hand upon his shoulder.

Waleran watched, with a smile as hideous as the open mouth of a dying snake. "Please," Waleran said to Thomas through that smile. "Save us both time and effort and tell me of what we seek."

Katherine took an involuntary look at the open chest at the side of the cave. She quickly looked away again, but not soon enough.

"Ho!" Waleran said. "Something I should not see?"

He strode to the torch, pulled it from its base, and walked to the chest.

"A single book?" Disappointment registered in his voice.

"We have been searching for ten years for the great treasure that Lord Baldwin had heard was rumored to appear among the Merlins, and all I find is a single book?"

"It is nothing," Thomas said quickly. "What you seek lies at the bottom of the pond."

"Play no games with me," Waleran warned Thomas. "Your whimpering voice tells me perhaps this book *is* valuable."

"I would rather die than tell you."

"Tell him all, Thomas," Sir William said. "Mayhaps we can leave with our lives . . ."

"Yes," Waleran said in oily tones. "Tell all."

Thomas blinked once, twice, as if trying to decide.

"Spare yourselves further agony," Waleran said. "And tell me of this book." Waleran's voice rose in volume with such impatience that the baby woke and began to cry.

"Shut that whelp's mouth!" he ordered the nurse.

"No," the nurse whispered calmly.

"No? No?" Waleran's face began to purple with sudden rage. "You dare defy me? A common peasant dare defy the Duke of Whittingham? Master of the Druids? The right hand man of King Edward the Second? You defy me?"

The nurse lifted her head and pushed the shawl away from her face.

"*I* defy *you?*" she asked as she stared Waleran directly in the face. "Ask instead if *you* dare defy me?"

Waleran staggered backward. "Queen Isabella!"

"Indeed," she said. "The one person in England that King Edward trusts more than you, his beloved Duke of Whittingham. And I have heard enough for you to hang."

She smiled.

"And enough for the Druids to be wiped from the face of the earth."

20

"Impossible," Waleran said. The slate gray color of his face showed, however, that he believed it all too possible. "How . . . how. . . . "

Queen Isabella stood, and gracefully moved to Katherine while Waleran's jaw worked against empty air.

Katherine accepted the offered baby with awe, and hugged it warm against her chest.

The Queen of England and . . . and the future king in my arms. Surely I dream.

"How is it I am here—the last place on earth a traitor like you would expect?" Queen Isabella drew to her full height. Her words were ice—brittle and unforgiving.

The peasant's shawl was still wrapped around her, but her posture became unmistakably royal. Her back was now straight, shoulders now squared, and chin held high with dignity. The pale, smooth skin of her face was not coarsened like that of most peasants from exposure to sun or wind, and that skin sharply contrasted her dark, thick hair and full red lips. An aura seemed to grow around her as she once again became the woman accustomed to the power of life and death over thousands of her subjects.

She fixed her terrible gaze on Waleran and advanced. "I am here because of a mysterious stranger who appeared in the royal bedchambers shortly before dawn barely a fortnight ago."

Waleran shook his head as he retreated until his back touched the cave wall. "No. Only one man would be capable of such a thing, and he is dead."

"His ghost, then, appeared," Queen Isabella said without smiling. "And at first, I believed it to be a ghost. How else could a mere man slip through the royal residence and avoid the guards."

"But—"

"My first impulse was to scream. Yet something about the man's calmness . . ." Queen Isabella smiled in recollection. "This man informed me that my son Edward had been taken. King Edward was at the country estate, and I was alone except for the guards roaming the castle. But I did not panic. There was a gentleness about this man. . . ."

Waleran began to shake, a dog waiting to be beaten.

"This man invited me to see for myself if the baby was gone, and said he would be waiting for my return to the royal chambers. He was not afraid, this man, for he said if he had lied, then I could call the guards. He told me if baby Edward truly had been taken, however, it would be in my best interest to hear the story. The baby was gone from the nursery, and I returned without calling alarm. And listened."

Baby Edward began to cry. Katherine rocked him, but to no avail.

"That mysterious stranger informed me that dawn of a plot against the throne," Queen Isabella said. "A Druid plot

Understandably, I found the thought ridiculous. Druids were a myth, superstition, I told him."

Katherine concentrated on the boy in her arms. But the boy sensed her strangeness and still cried for his mother.

Queen Isabella turned away from Waleran and held out her arms for the baby.

"Sir William," she said over her shoulder, "My son needs me. If you would care to finish."

"With pleasure, m'lady."

Katherine noticed Sir William had again withdrawn his sword. So engrossed had she been in the baby, she could not say when it had happened.

"Waleran, or . . ." Sir William paused as he lifted the sword, "would you prefer the title Duke Whittingham, short-lived as I pray that title may be?"

Waleran sank until he was sitting, back against the wall.

"We knew that someone, somewhere, in the royal court was a Druid," Sir William said. "Thomas and Katherine were sent merely to force that Druid—you to little surprise—into action. We knew that it would be of utmost importance to prevent the slightest hint of Druids to reach the king's ear."

Waleran groaned. "You fully expected Katherine and Thomas to be thrown into the Tower."

Sir William nodded.

Katherine smiled a tight smile of relief to be alive. There had been little joy and much fear in her heart as they waited for a royal audience, knowing that execution may have easily been the result instead of a mere prison sentence. But they had also gambled on more, something else that Katherine now could have related just as easily as did the knight.

"Waleran," Sir William said, "Not once, but twice against us did you rely on knowledge gained from conversations overheard in prison. In Magnus while you yourself sat among Thomas and I. And in York, next to the Earl himself. Once too you used the trick of letting a foe escape, simply to follow. We thought it likely the same ploy would be used again."

"You knew I was the king's chamberlain?"

Sir William shook his head. "Thomas' father suspected. He had been traveling England for years as an old man."

"No!" Again a flash of fear. "I tell you, he is dead."

A tall man walked into the cave from where he had been waiting in the shadows of the entrance.

"If I am dead," he replied to Waleran, "then let me be your most persistent nightmare."

Waleran moaned. "I thought you dead when we conquered Magnus. Later, I knew you traveled in disguise, but I thought I'd finally beaten you outside York, when Thomas led my soldiers to your campsite."

"I am most definitely alive." The man bowed to Queen Isabella. "Your Majesty . . ."

She smiled in return.

And how could she not help but smile, Katherine thought. *For this man is as handsome as his son Thomas, with the same hint of mystery and confidence, the same air of gentleness and compassion.*

"Lord Hawkwood," she said. "I am pleased to discover my trust in you was not misplaced."

"It was a near thing, was it not? For a moment, you nearly impaled me."

Waleran now had his arms huddled around his knees. "I-impaled?" he managed to stutter.

The baby was quiet now, and Queen Isabella turned her attention again to Waleran.

Katherine caught the instant transition from the warmth directed to Lord Hawkwood to the hatred and cold reserve for Waleran.

"Lord Hawkwood offered to place his life in my hands. In my royal chambers that dawn, he opened my palm, set the handle of a short dagger upon my skin, closed my fingers over the dagger, and brought my hand up so that the dagger touched his throat. He told me if I chose to disbelieve him, I could end his life right there. But if I believed, I was to arrange for a trip into the countryside, as if distraught over the kidnapping, and instead, unknown to King Edward, attend my own son here, while we waited."

"For me," Waleran blurted. "You expected me to arrive."

Katherine cleared her throat. "Yes. Thomas shouted at the entrance to this valley. We feared you might not have managed to follow. Then we waited at the river by the abbey, once again giving you time. Finally, we talked loudly in front of the entrance to this very cave. All to lure you inside."

Waleran lifted his head. An animal-like gleam, almost of insanity, suddenly filled his eyes.

"My army outside! I may die here, but you cannot escape."

"You no longer have an army outside." By the softness of Thomas' words, Katherine knew Thomas felt pity for the completeness of their enemy's destruction.

"We expected you, did we not?" Thomas asked. "Many more than twenty of the finest men of Magnus were hidden in these woods. Your army has long since fallen to ambush during our time in this cave."

21

They gathered—the five of them and baby Edward—in the abbey hall that evening.

Queen Isabella was given the chair closest to the fire. She and the baby were wrapped in blankets, for although it was July, the evening chill in this northern valley had a bite, especially in an abbey hall with a cold stone floor and no luxurious tapestries to slow any drafts.

Sir William was pacing the room slowly, a man of coiled energy still restless after the day's events, even with Waleran and his army safely captured.

Lord Hawkwood sat crouched on his knees, poking an iron into the fire to rearrange the burning wood.

Katherine and Thomas sat next to each other, opposite Queen Isabella.

They had all gathered here at the request of the queen, who had spent the bulk of the afternoon chatting with the men of Magnus, much to their delight. Now, however, Queen Isabella wasted little time in idle conversation.

"What will draw the remaining Druid leaders to this valley?" The question was asked softly, yet Katherine sensed the steel behind it.

"Your majesty?" Lord Hawkwood expressed puzzlement without shifting from his position near the fire.

"I have agreed to give as many men as you deem necessary to capture all the Druids who arrive in the next weeks, but I wish to know what they seek."

Sir William stopped his pacing, and stood behind Thomas.

It *is* the book, in that cave, I believe," Queen Isabella continued. "And you all seek to avoid the subject. I find it both amusing and strange that so much has been revealed about the Druids, and so little about yourselves. Merlins."

She smiled, but it did not rob the strength of her implied command to tell her all.

Lord Hawkwood prodded the fire again and did not flinch as sparks shot from a falling log. He took his time to add several more logs, then rose and faced Queen Isabella.

"You see the last of the Merlins here in this room," he said without self-pity, "so there is little to say about us."

Katherine held her breath. *Would Queen Isabella press the issue?*

Lord Hawkwood continued smoothly. "However, as you have guessed, it is the book which is of utmost importance."

"You have a habit of intriguing me," Queen Isabella said. "Please, go on."

Sir William stood. "I have brought the book from the trunk in the cave. Perhaps now is the time to deliver it to her majesty."

When Lord Hawkwood nodded, Sir Willam left the room, and Lord Hawkwood closed his eyes to think as he spoke. "It begins with an explorer named Marco Polo . . ."

"Yes." Queen Isabella nodded. "The name is familiar. He

dictated a book—*Description of the World,* I believe—while in prison."

"It is remarkable you know that," Lord Hawkwood said, eyes now open. "His book is only gaining popularity now."

"Not remarkable at all. Coincidence. The man who transcribed the dictation, a romance writer named Rustichello of Pisa, spent time under the patronage of King Edward, my father-in-law. Royal courts all over Europe have copies of this book."

Lord Hawkwood grinned. "Then, m'lady, you shall readily understand what follows. As you know, Marco Polo explored Cathay, the unknown lands of the Far East. His patron was the Great Kublai Khan, ruler of the Mongols. Polo received a golden passport from Khan, and for twenty years he traveled safely through that land, recording everything he saw."

Queen Isabella nodded impatiently. "He beheld wonders, to be sure. I am told the people there have yellow skin and slanted eyes and are extremely intelligent."

She waited while Sir William rejoined them, a large, leather bound sheaf of parchments in his hand.

"But what," she asked, "has Marco Polo to do with *your* book here, a book to draw Druids like flies to honey."

"Consider this, your majesty. What if Polo recorded other books, not merely fanciful tales of the exotic, but books with the most advanced science of this world, books with secrets so powerful that kingdoms might rise and fall upon them?"

"I find that difficult to believe."

Lord Hawkwood turned to Thomas. "Please bring some of the exploding powder."

Thomas left silently, and returned several minutes later with a small leather bag. Lord Hawkwood reached in and removed a pinched portion of dark powder.

"Potassium, your majesty," he explained. "Sulfur and charcoal. Ingredients easily obtained."

Lord Hawkwood poured a tiny trail of the powder onto the floor, near the fireplace. He twisted a twig loose from a nearby log, held the twig in the fire until it was lit, then touched that small flame to the line of powder.

Even though Katherine knew what to expect, she still marveled at the small flaring explosion of light and sound.

Lord Hawkwood turned back to Queen Isabella. His face was blackened with smudge.

Queen Isabella did not laugh, however. Her eyes were still wide with wonder.

"Yes," Lord Hawkwood said. "Exploding powder. The people of Cathay invented it centuries ago. Yet we in Europe have no knowledge of it. And Marco Polo deliberately left it from his descriptions of that land. For good reason. Imagine the possibilities. If such power would be harnessed by men of evil. . . ."

"It saved our lives," Thomas said.

Queen Isabella shifted her eyes to him.

"In the Holy Land," Thomas said. "Father had lined a pit with it. When it flared in the darkness, all the bandits panicked. We succeeded in our attack."

Queen Isabella nodded. "I think I understand. This book of yours, if it contains more such secrets, would be as valuable as a kingdom."

Then she asked sharply. "How is it that you have it?"

"The Roman church—in Polo's homeland of Italy, of course—had confiscated it for fear of what it might accomplish and destroy," Lord Hawkwood answered. "In my own travels after the fall of Magnus, I heard rumors of it, and. . . ."

Lord Hawkwood appealed to the Queen. "I would prefer not to say how it was obtained, only that I had it sent here, to this abbey, where Thomas was to be raised away from the eyes of Druids. He would need what he learned from the book to regain Magnus."

"I will not press you for that secret," Queen Isabella said. "There is enough pain in your eyes and you are a man of honor."

Lord Hawkwood nodded thanks.

"And the book is now mine?" Queen Isabella asked.

"If you wish," Lord Hawkwood replied.

"Why would I not wish?"

"If it falls into the wrong hands . . ." Lord Hawkwood struggled for words. "Knowledge of such a book will drive many men to desperate measures to obtain it. And in the wrong hands, a civilization may be shattered."

Lord Hawkwood began to pace, much as Sir William had done earlier. "Examine the politics of Europe. The balances of power are so delicately held. Your husband may choose to take the secrets of this book and fight more than just the Scots. Other kings may begin wars to obtain your knowledge. After all, men have fought before for much less reason. Even this exploding powder can kill men by the dozens, while ordinary warfare is much more kind."

He pointed at the baby sleeping in Queen Isabella's arms. "Too many die to leave the fatherless behind. Perhaps we can delay the advance of knowledge which might be used by evil men."

Queen Isabella stared at Lord Hawkwood and said nothing.

The fire crackled and popped several times in the silence.

"You have done so much for us," she said. "King Edward, of course, will end the Druid uprising. In secrecy, of course. It would do little good for the people to be stirred by these matters."

She hugged her baby. "You have ensured my son will

inherit a kingdom, that revolt will not tear this land apart. And now, you offer this book—I presume not copied by any hands."

"You presume correctly," Lord Hawkwood said.

Queen Isabella looked from one to the other. Silently gazing first at Katherine, then Thomas, then Sir William and finally, Lord Hawkwood.

"Because of this secrecy, history will not record what you have accomplished. And that fills me with sadness. You are worthy of much more."

She nodded at the book. "And we will engage in this final act of secrecy."

Several more heartbeats.

"Thomas," Queen Isabella then said softly. "Cast the book into the fire."

THOMAS
Quest Fulfilled

LATE SUMMER A. D. 1314

"Contrary to what you might think," Lord Hawkwood smiled at Thomas, "we are not ready to depart this abbey for Magnus."

Thomas innocently raised an eyebrow. "Oh? Queen Isabella was satisfied that no more Druid leaders will arrive. Surely there remains nothing for us here."

Father gazed at son.

They stood along the river in front of the abbey hall. Midmorning sun warmed their backs. They shared the feeling of peace given by a valley quiet of wind, quiet except for the distant lowing of cattle and occasional bleat of sheep.

Much had been accomplished. Day after day in the last two weeks, solitary travelers had arrived in the valley. Without fail, when captured, each had pleaded innocent to the charges of Druid conspiracy, but Waleran—as part of a desperate bargain to save his own life—had identified each as a Druid.

The full horror of the Druid secret circle had been exposed

in those two weeks. Again and again, Queen Isabella had murmured shock and surprise to face each new arriving Druid. Many she knew from their positions of power in society. Magistrates, sheriffs, priests, knights and even earls and dukes.

All were now stripped of their worldly wealth and safely imprisoned. In one swoop, most of the Druids across the land had been taken.

Beyond that, Queen Isabella had pledges to begin action against remaining Druids who falsely posed as priests in the northern towns. Not only would the spread of their power be contained, but the base they had established in the last few years would be totally eliminated.

"Thomas," Lord Hawkwood said in a mock-stern voice. "Were you raised a Merlin?"

Thomas grinned and nodded. He enjoyed knowing he could not—even in jest—fool the man in front of him.

Strange, he thought, *to one day suddenly be forced to consider a stranger as flesh-and-blood father. Especially a man accustomed to shrouding himself in mystery.*

Yet the bond had formed. And Thomas felt himself flushing at the implied compliment.

"Yes. I was raised a Merlin," Thomas replied.

"Tell me then—instead of pretending ignorant innocence in hopes of hearing me prattle—why is it that we are not ready to depart?"

Thomas looked beyond his father's shoulder at the high walls of the abbey. At the tiny window that he had so often used for escape in the days he believed he was an orphan.

"We are not yet ready to depart, because there does remain something for us here. Something we could not seek until Queen Isabella departed, for she should not know of it."

"Ummn." Lord Hawkwood was noncommittal.

Thomas grinned again in pleasure. *Like before. In his childhood. Exercises of the mind. Tests of logic.*

"Sarah would have enjoyed this." The words came from his mouth even as they reached his thoughts.

Thomas stopped, suddenly awkward. Always, deep inside, there was the ache that Sarah was gone.

"I grieve too," Lord Hawkwood said in the lengthening silence. "Perhaps that is the highest tribute. To never be forgotten."

For several minutes, each stood without speaking, in the companionable way that friends develop when comfort replaces the need to fill air with words.

Then a tiny roe deer moved from the nearby trees, hesitant at first, then confident that it was alone. Thomas clapped, and the deer scrambled sideways so quickly it almost fell.

The effect was so comical that each snorted with laughter.

"Life," Lord Hawkwood then said. "The past should not prevent us from looking ahead and drinking fully from life, from enjoying each moment as it arrives."

Thomas let out a deep breath. "Yes."

"And one looks forward to drinking deeply this cup with Katherine?"

Thomas coughed. "Our reason for delaying departure," he said quickly. "You were testing my observations."

Lord Hawkwood graciously did not pursue the subject of Katherine, and instead nodded.

"There had to be more reason for the Druids to arrive here than a single book," Thomas said. "For many of these men, it involved the risk of travel and the need to explain a lengthy absence. No, there must be more."

"An interesting theory," Lord Hawkwood said. "What might you guess?"

"Before I answer," Thomas challenged, "I have my own question for you."

Lord Hawkwood waited.

"What," Thomas began, "is the single most powerful weapon available to men?"

"Not swords."

Thomas nodded.

"Not arrows. Not catapults"

Thomas nodded again.

"Not any physical means of destruction. For with the invention of each new weapon, there will be a countering defense."

"So . . ." Thomas bantered.

"So, as you full well know, my son, our greatest power is knowledge. In warfare. In business. In the affairs of our own lives. In the defense of our faith. Without knowledge, we are nothing."

Thomas pointed at the tiny window high on the abbey wall. "Were we to wager today my odds of answering your question, I would have an unfair advantage. For last night, as I puzzled yet again what might draw so many Druids to this valley, I returned to the bedchamber of my childhood."

Lord Hawkwood straightened with sudden interest. "You have not discovered. . . ."

Thomas grinned mischief. "Ho, ho! The student knows something the teacher does not. Surely you speak truth that knowledge is power!"

"Thomas, tell me!"

Thomas bent to scoop pebbles into his hand. One by one, he began to toss them into the tiny river.

"Thomas . . ." Lord Hawkwood warned.

"In the Holy Land," Thomas said, "Sir William informed me that I held the final secrets to the battle. Yet—" Thomas pointed his forefinger skyward for emphasis—"I had no inkling of what he might mean."

Thomas tossed two more pebbles into the water before continuing. "Sir William had returned from exile in the Holy Land to spend time in Magnus with me," he said. "Had the final secrets been there, he would have claimed it then. Moreover, had this mysterious object of great value been there, the Druids, who held Magnus for a generation, would have claimed it. Instead, since my departure from this abbey, both sides—Druid and Merlin—have been intent on learning the secret from me, a secret I did not know I possessed. I can only conclude that whatever it was, has lain here at the abbey."

Lord Hawkwood nodded.

"Indeed," Thomas continued, "if you yourself do not know where at this abbey it is located, I must conclude that it had been sent to Sarah, along with the book she chose to hide in the cave."

Again, Lord Hawkwood nodded.

"Whatever this secret was," Thomas concluded, "Sarah hid it before her death. Whatever this secret was, the Druids were willing—no, desperate enough—to each undertake a journey from their separate parts of England."

Thomas smiled. "Returning here to the abbey brought back to me some of my first memories of Sarah. I remember now, that she would sit beside my bed and help me with my prayers or sing quiet songs of knights performing valiant deeds. And every night, her final words as I fell to sleep never differed."

His focus shifted from the edge of the valley hills to his father's face.

"Sarah would say, 'Thomas, my love, sleep upon the winds of light.' Each night, she would simply smile when I asked what that meant."

Lord Hawkwood began to smile too.

"Yes," Thomas said. "Your words to me at the gallows—now it seems so long ago—as a mysterious man, hidden beneath cloak and hood, were almost the same."

"Bring the winds of light," Lord Hawkwood's voice was almost a whisper, "into this age of darkness."

"Knowledge," Thomas said. "The knowledge accumulated by generations of Merlins."

"Yes, Thomas," Lord Hawkwood said. "Merlin himself founded Magnus as a place to conduct our hidden warfare against the Druids. Yet he destined us for more. To search the world for what men knew. And to save that knowledge from the darkness of the destruction of barbarians."

Lord Hawkwood's voice became sad. "Time and again throughout history, gentle scholars have suffered loss to men of swords. Great libraries have been burned and looted, the records of civilizations and their accomplishments and advances wiped from the face of the earth. Few today know of the wondrous pyramids of the ancient Egyptians, of the math and astronomy of the ancient Greeks, of the healing medicines of, yes, the Druids, of the aqueducts and roads of the Romans."

In a flash, Thomas understood. "Merlins of each generation traveled the world and returned with written record of what they discovered. . . ."

"When Magnus fell," Lord Hawkwood said, "it was more important than our lives to save the books which contained this knowledge. That is why so many of us died. Your mother and I, Sir William, and a few others escaped with the books of these centuries of knowledge, while the rest gave their lives. Why did each Druid willingly undertake a journey here when given the message by Waleran? Each assumed, rightly, there would be spoils easily divided. Books beyond value. One, two perhaps more books for each. Books which can only be duplicated through years of transcribing."

"Father," Thomas said quickly, because now, seeing the worry on his father's face, he found no joy in prolonging his news, "the books you sent to this abbey are safe."

"Yes?"

"Sleep upon the winds of light," Thomas said. "What better place to hide something than in the open? My mattress was placed upon a great trunk, placed so that its edges hid the sight of the lid of the trunk. A passerby, or even a searcher, of course, would think it only a convenient pedestal to keep a sleeping child away from nighttime rats. But within that trunk . . . each night I truly did sleep upon the winds of light."

23

Thomas, on his knees, thrilled to the touch of the sword atop his shoulder.

It was a private and quiet ceremony in the uppermost chambers of the castle of Magnus, with Sir William, Lord Hawkwood and, of course, Katherine, who held the sword.

"This is our own form of knighthood," she said softly. "An unseen badge of honor."

"It is enough," Thomas replied as he rose. "Worth more than the knighthood granted by Queen Isabella, more than this kingdom officially given us by her royal charter."

Thomas felt a sorrow, however, for just as the continued existence of Merlins had been kept from Queen Isabella, so too must he keep this part of his life hidden from those who waited below in the great hall to begin a feast of homecoming for him.

Tiny John, now bigger than the rascal sprout he remembered before exile. Robert of Uleran, the valiant sheriff of Magnus who had survived his imprisonment and resisted all promises of the Druid priests. The Earl of York, joyful to have his earldom returned. Gervase, a man of simple faith who had oft comforted Thomas and provided him escape from Magnus at the price of a barely survived terrible beating by the Druid high priests. And, a magnificent dog—the puppy Thomas had taken across half a world, then taken back again from St. Jean d'Acre.

"Our task is not complete," Lord Hawkwood interrupted Thomas' thoughts. "For should we choose, there is always the search for the Holy Grail, which disappeared when you fled York. And I cannot believe that the Druid circle will not somehow, sometime, begin to rebuild."

He smiled. "But—I believe—we as Merlins will now be able to continue our task. Searching and keeping the treasures of knowledge. And passing on that task to future generations."

His voice became fuller as he spoke with growing passion. "There will be a day," he said, "when a renaissance, a rebirth of the sharing of ideas will take all of us forward into the dawning of a better age. Until then, let us ensure that Magnus stands, quiet, unknown, and on guard against the age of darkness."

Sir William, unexpectedly, began to laugh. "Well spoken, Lord Hawkwood," he finally said through a broad smile. "But first we need future generations. And *I* will not see our task complete until you and I become grandfathers."

Katherine giggled.

Thomas felt his jaw gape open. *To be sure,* he thought in confusion, *Katherine and I have pledged marriage, but we had not yet spoken of children. . . .*

Then another thought struck him.

"What is this of which you speak?" he blurted to Sir William. "If—"

"When," Katherine corrected.

"When," Thomas said, "our marriage results in . . . in . . . little ones, it strikes me that Lord Hawkwood alone will become a grandfather. Who is it that *you,* Sir William, expect to arrive with a babe in swaddling clothes to provide a grandchild?"

Lord Hawkwood began to laugh in great gales. Sir William joined him, then Katherine.

Thomas fought bewilderment.

Finally, he roared his words to be heard above the laughter.

"What is it?"

Sir William found his voice.

"Thomas," he said. "You showed such insight into the untangling of the past, we all assumed you already knew."

"Knew what?" Thomas snapped. Mirth had reddened all their faces, and he did not enjoy being the source of their laughter.

Sir William moved closer and embraced him, then stood back.

"Thomas," he said. "Katherine is my daughter. Born, as you were, during exile in the Holy Land."

"But . . . but . . . " Thomas sputtered.

"Yes," Sir William said. "It will be I who gives her hand away in marriage as you two begin to reign Magnus. And Thomas?"

"Yes?"

"I could not think of another man I would welcome more as my son than Thomas, Lord and Earl of Magnus."

HISTORICAL NOTES

Readers may find it of interest that in the times in which the "Winds of Light" series is set, children were considered adults much earlier than now. By church law, for example, a bride had to be at least 12, a bridegroom 14. (This suggests that upon occasion, marriage occurred at an even earlier age!)

It is not so unusual then, to think of Thomas of Magnus becoming accepted as a leader by the age of 16; many would already consider him a man simply because of his age. Moreover, other "men" also became leaders at remarkably young ages during those times. King Richard II, for example, was only 14 years old when he rode out to face the leaders of the Peasants' Revolt in 1381.

Chapter One

Jerusalem's history stretches back for more than 3,500 years. Its fortified walls were destroyed by invaders more than once; the last occasion because of the orders of the Roman emperor Titus, in the year A.D. 70 because of the first Jewish rebellion against the Roman Empire. After the fall of the Roman Empire, Jerusalem passed into the rule of the religiously tolerant Muslims, fell again to the knights of the First Crusade in 1099, was taken back by the Mamelukes who rebuilt the walls and restored much of the city.

Thomas fears **crucifixion** with good reason. His thoughts on the method of this horrible death are historically accurate. Readers of the Gospels will also know that there was a custom of breaking the legs of the victims to hasten death of anyone who survived a day on the cross.

The Crusades were a series of religious wars from the years A.D. 1095. (The First Crusade) to 1270 (the Eighth Crusade). These wars were organized by European powers to recover from Muslims (infidels) the Christian holy places in Palestine, especially the Holy City: Jerusalem. Many of the Crusaders believed that if they died in battle, their souls would be taken straight to heaven.

Gradually, toward the end of the 1200s, the Muslims reconquered all the cities which had been taken from them. St. Jean d'Acre, the common destination for all ships bearing Crusaders, was the last to fall to the Muslims, and remained in Christian hands until the year A.D. 1291.

A warrior race of Muslim Egypt, **Mamelukes** were originally non-Arab slaves to Egyptian rulers. They overthrew their rulers in middle of the 1200s. Not only did they prove to be too powerful for the Crusaders, they were the only people to ever defeat a Mongol invasion—in the year A.D. 1260.

Chapter Two

Often readers of the Old Testament forget how historically

accurate is its accounting of Jewish history, as proven where modern day archeology has succeeded in discovering the sites of such events. King David's assault on **Gihon Spring** is reported in the Old Testament (2 Sam. 5:6-10). While it is reasonable to assume that any occupants of Jerusalem since then would guard *against* another such assault; it should not be surprising that defenders might forget the spring could also serve as an exit.

Chapter Three
Thomas shows an excellent sense of logic as he notes the well's walls become narrower at the top. As ancient cities aged throughout the centuries, garbage and rubble contributed to the slow building up of the ground. Some excavations today reach 30-40 feet deep to reveal life of the past at certain "layers" of time.

Chapter Five
The earliest known records of **Druids** come from the third century B.C., and according to the Roman general Julius Caesar (who is the principle source of today's information on Druids), this group of men studied ancient verse, natural philosophy, astronomy, and the lore of the gods. The principal doctrine of the Druids was that souls passed at death from one person to another.

Druids offered human victims for those who were in danger of death in battle or who were gravely ill. They sacrificed these victims by burning them in huge wickerwork images.

As mentioned in the letter of chapter 18 the Druids were suppressed in ancient Britain by the Roman conquerors in the first century A.D. If indeed the cult survived, it must have had to remain as secret as it was during Thomas' time.

Today, followers of the Druid cult may still be found in

England worshiping the ancient ruins of Stonehenge at certain times of the year.

Sir William's fear of a small group of men taking control to bring evil upon an entire country is not unfounded, especially in light of horrible events of recent history. Adolf Hitler, for example, as a single leader atop a pyramid of power, delivered and preached a message of racial hatred that managed to manipulate thousands upon thousands of ordinary people into assisting in the murder of millions of innocent Jews.

Probably because of an excellent education, Sir William is acutely accurate in his observation of the **Dark Ages,** the term commonly given to the years A.D. 500–1000. These were centuries of decline across Europe, mostly attributed to the fall of the Roman Empire which left a vacuum of power that encouraged civil wars and stifled classical culture. This lack of education among the common people and the suspicion between countries prevented the sharing of ideas, especially in the arts, science, navigation, and medicine. (Interestingly enough, what culture there was remained preserved in remnants by monks of Ireland, Italy, France, and Britain.) Not until the **Renaissance**—A.D. 1350–1650—did modern civilization begin to flourish as men across Europe began again to strive to learn and share ideas.

Chapter Seven

Historical record shows that the **Second Jewish Revolt** took place in A.D. 132 and lasted for three and a half years. **Cassius Dio,** a Roman historian as noted in the letter, wrote a brief notice of the war which has survived to this day. In this notice, Dio relates that toward the end of the rebellion, Roman legionaires were unable to engage the Jews in open battle because of the rough terrain, and instead were forced to hunt them down in small groups in the caves which they hid, and starve them out. Cassius Dio describes the final results this way: "Fifty of their [Jews] most important outposts and nine hundred and eighty-five of their most famous villages were razed to the ground. Five hundred and eighty thousand men were slain in the various raids and battles, and the number of those who perished from famine, disease and fire was past finding out. Thus nearly the whole of Judea was made desolate."

As also noted in the letter, the Roman general **Julius Severus** *was* summoned from Britain to end the rebellion. Despite the fact that the timing of Druid disappearance and the stolen treasure is so close as to be possibly regarded as more than coincidental, there have been found no historical notes regarding a Druid treasure. A number of the mentioned Dead Sea caves, however, were discovered in 1951–52 and 1960–61.

Chapter Ten
It is not unreasonable to assume **The Cave of Letters** would lay undiscovered for the centuries from the time of Roman general Julius Severus until entered by Thomas and the bandits. No mention of the treasure is found in historical documents—but Mameluke soldiers would have had great incentive to keep the discovery of such great wealth to themselves. That the caves could be so well hidden and unknown is demonstrated by the fact that modern archeologists did not discover these sites until five centuries more had passed, in the years 1951–52 and 1960–61. Among the artifacts found in these caves were a basket of skulls, keys, metal vessels,

parchment of palms, and fish net. Among all the caves, at least 60 skeletons were found.

Chapter Eleven
In the first book of the "Winds of Light" series, *Wings of an Angel,* Thomas uses **gunpowder** to his advantage.

Chapter Thirteen
Readers may find it interesting that the courtier's promised **"ten minutes of audience"** was in those times a relatively new term. With the arrival of mechanical clocks at end of the 1200's and the beginning of the 1300's, mankind, for the first time in history, had found a way to impose regularity upon time; until then, an "hour" could only be measured as a portion of daylight, which of course varied from season to season. By finally establishing an "equal hour," man gained control over the daily measure of time, and a "minute" first became a divided portion of that hour.

Chapter Fourteen
England's battles against **Scotland,** were begun by King Edward the First (who was recalled from the Holy Land earlier at the news of his father's death) in A.D. 1296. King Edward the Second did continue those battles to little avail. Shortly before Thomas and Katherine appeared in London for a royal audience, Edward the Second had lost a disastrous battle against the Scots at Bannockburn. The politics of that time would have put great pressure on Edward the Second for this loss; it is no wonder that he might have had little grasp on domestic affairs. Scotland, unlike Ireland or Wales, never did succumb to the English. A truce was declared in 1323. The poison contained in all parts of the **rhododendron,** an evergreen shrub common in all parts of Britain, is carbohy-

drate andormedotoxin. While normally it takes over an hour for its poison to work, it is not unlikely that other herbs were added to compound its affect. Both Druids and the historical Merlins were famed for their knowledge of the poisons and medicines of plants and unfortunately, little of what they actually knew has survived.

Chapter Eighteen

There is no historical mention of Edward the Third's brief kidnapping. However, especially given the ultimatum by Edward the Second to put pressure on his political enemies, it might be possible that King Edward did not want to alarm the people of England during a time of instability made worse by his recent losses to Scotland. King Edward, then, logically would have hoped to gain his son back without public knowledge of either the kidnapping or return. And, given the briefness of Edward the Third's disappearance, and Queen Isabella's involvement, it is perhaps understandable that historians are unaware of such an event.

Chapter Nineteen

Queen Isabella, the daughter of France's Phillip IV, married King Edward the Second in 1308, and gave birth to Edward the Third on November 13, 1312. Isabella later joined forces with Roger de Mortimer, the first Earl of March, and they forced Edward the Second's abdication of the throne in 1327 to give power to Edward the Third. Ironically, Edward the Third later rebelled against Mortimer's power and had him executed.

Chapter Twenty-One

Marco Polo, who left for Cathay (China) in the year 1271 with his father and uncle, was reputed to have a photographic memory. Because of that, the intensely curious and open-minded emperor Kublai Khan appointed Polo as an envoy, diplomat, and observer of an empire that covered half the known world.

For twenty years—protected by Khan's "golden passport"—Polo explored the culture, politics, and science of one of history's most dazzling, yet secluded empires.

Long given up for dead, he was barely recognized when he returned to Venice with a fortune in jewels sewn into his clothing. Later, as a rich merchant, he was taken hostage in a sea war between Italian cities. From prison, he dictated a book of his recollections. (This book inspired Columbus to sail for the new world nearly two centuries later.)

To the disbelievers—those who scoffed at his tall tales—Marco Polo insisted, even on his death bed that he "... never told the half of what he saw."

Yet what if he *had* told the other half? His first book led Columbus to discover a new world. Historians might find it curious that gunpowder—if used by the Chinese for four centuries before Polo's arrival there—is not mentioned in the published book. Yet, coincidentally or not, gunpowder was "invented" in Germany, shortly after Polo returned from China. Does this suggest that some of Polo's knowledge was not made public, but rather was described in other missing or stolen books of his voyages?

~ The Winds of Light ~		~ Historical Overview ~	
* 54 BC	Roman soldiers first enter Britain; by 43 A.D., Romans had conquered enough to establish London	* 1291 AD	St. Jean d'Acre, last stronghold of the Crusaders, falls to Muslim infidels in Holy Land
† 100 AD	Druid high priests form secret circle to avoid persecution by conquering Romans	* 1296	King Edward I begins wars against Scotland; wars are continued by Edward II, end in truce in 1323
* 132	Julius Severus sent from Britain to quell Second Jewish revolt in progress in Roman-held Holy Lands	† 1298	Thomas born to exiled parents in Holy Land; several months later, Katherine born there to her parents
* 300	Possible beginning of legend of Holy Grail and resulting quests for its existence	* 1299	Marco Polo in Genoa, Italy jail because of merchant war; dictates travel book to writer also in same jail
* 436	Last Roman troops leave Britain; Anglo-Saxon reign begins	* 1301	'Description of the World' — title later changed to 'The Travels of Marco Polo' — reaches European public
* 530	Anglo-Saxon King Arthur establishes Knights of the Round Table — as agreed upon by some historians	† 1303	Sarah takes son Thomas to English monastery; husband Lord Hawkwood roam England in disguise as old man
† 540	Merlin abandons Druid secret circle; establishes Magnus in remote moors of North England	† 1303	Lord Hawkwood arranges for Marco Polo's 'other' books to be sent to Sarah at English monastery
* 792	First Viking town established in Britain; beginning of end of Anglo-Saxon reign	* 1307	King Eward II begins reign as King of England; loses series of battles against Scotland until truce in 1323
* 1000	By this time, the Chinese have perfected their invention of gunpowder; used for fireworks	* 1308	Isabella, daughter of French king Phillip IV, marries King Edward II; Edward III born, Nov. 13, 1312
* 1066	Norman (French) knights win decisive Battle of Hastings; become new conquers of England	† 1309	Sarah dies at monastery; Thomas not yet told of Merlins
* 1095	Pope Urban II proclaims the First Crusade; Europeans embark on wars to win Holy Land	† 1312	Thomas first reconquers Magnus; as described in *Wings of An Angel, Barbarians From The Isle*
* 1270	Eighth (and final) Crusade begins; castles & kingdoms have been long established in Holy Land	† 1313	Thomas exiled from Magnus, flees to Holy Land: *Legend of Burning Water, The Forsaken Crusade, City of Dreams*
* 1271	Marco Polo — aged 17 — departs Italy for China with father and uncle; the trip takes nearly four years	† 1314	Thomas, Sir William, Katherine and Lord Hawkwood return to England from Holy Land: *Merlin's Destiny*
† 1290	Magnus falls to Druids; Sir William, Lord Hawkwood flee to Holy Land	* 1317	gunpowder commonly known in Europe; within two hundreds years, warfare changed completely

*** — denotes historical fact** **† — denotes author's historical speculation**